FULL HOUSE

FULL HOUSE

*TEN SHORT STORIES BY
EDGAR AWARD WINNING
MYSTERY WRITER*

DAVID HOUSEWRIGHT

DOWN&OUT
BOOKS

Down and Out Books, LLC
3959 Van Dyke Rd, Ste. 265
Lutz, FL 33558
www.DownAndOutBooks.com

Cover art and design by JT Lindroos

ISBN-10: 193749571X

ISBN-13:978-1-937495-71-8

CONTENTS

For Renée

Author's Note: This was my very first short story and features Holland Taylor, the traditional trench coat detective that appeared in my first three novels—PENANCE, winner of the 1996 Edgar Award for Best First Novel from the Mystery Writers of America; PRACTICE TO DECEIVE, 1998 Minnesota Book Award Winner; and DEARLY DEPARTED.

Kids Today

There were two stiffs on the floor and two kids soaked with blood standing over them and all the Minneapolis homicide cop wanted to know was: "What were you thinking, taking a teenage girl for a client without permission from her parents?"

"It seemed like a good idea at the time," I told him.

He looked the girl over. She had cradled her dead father until the cops pulled her off and his blood had stained her blonde hair, her cheeks, her shirt, her shorts, her long willowy legs, yet she remained impossibly beautiful.

"Yeah, I bet," the cop said and grinned.

"It was because she couldn't go to her parents that I took the job," I insisted. Only he wasn't listening. He knew my kind, sure he did. An over-stimulated, middle-aged private eye perfectly willing to risk license revocation for the opportunity to engage in unlawful sexual intercourse with a minor; happens all the time. Only that's not the way it was and I wanted him to know it. Course, in my defense

I could have mentioned the ten Ben Franklins she had dealt face-up on my desk blotter—a thousand bucks—but I didn't.

"Tell me about this," the cop said, gesturing toward the bloody scene. The mechanism that is a homicide investigation was in high gear and humming along. Officers in plain clothes and blues shot photographs, took measurements, examined blood stains and asked questions while the ME examined one of the bodies; I'd bet he couldn't wait to get to the other. In the opposite corner, two officers were standing on either side of a twenty-year-old white male, his blood-stained hands cuffed securely behind his back.

"I got the call about an hour ago," I said.

"From your client..." the cop inserted.

"Yeah, Rachel Hartman."

"The seventeen-year-old girl," he said, emphasizing seventeen.

I took a deep breath, chose to ignore the insinuation, continued.

"She told me she was afraid," I said.

"And you dropped everything and rushed right over," the cop said.

I nodded. A police woman was now at Rachel Hartman's side. She gently took the girl's elbow and ushered her away from the bodies to a chair on the far side of the living room.

"What was she afraid of?" the cop wanted to know.

"She wasn't clear. Something to do with her father and a gun."

"This gun?" he asked, holding up a 9mm Glock in a clear plastic bag.

I shrugged.

The cop's gaze drifted from one body to the other.

"Which one is her father?" he asked.

"They both are," I told him.

"Really," he said, expressing about as much surprise as if I had told him the Twins had dropped another one. "Care to introduce me?"

"This is Rachel's step-father, Steven Palke..." I said, pointing to the body on the far side of the room, the one whose face and chest had been turned to jelly by the shotgun.

"The millionaire computer entrepreneur," the cop added, expressing the unofficial title that would probably be attached to Palke's name in the obituaries.

"Uh huh. And this gentleman," I said, gesturing toward the older man with three ugly bullet holes in his chest, "is Rachel's birth father. Abe Hartman."

The cop's eyes widened. He knew Hartman's unofficial title, too.

"Abe 'the Cleaver' Hartman?" he asked.

"Yes."

"The gangster?"

"Yes."

"Yikes."

"You know, I said the very same thing when I was told."

"What the hell is going on?" the cop wanted to know. So I told him.

* * *

Earlier that day Rachel Hartman came through my office door like she had expected me to be waiting for her.

"Are you Holland Taylor, the private investigator?"

That's what it said on the name plate so I doubted she'd believe me if I told her I was Robert Mitchum; probably wouldn't know who Mitchum was anyway. She was dressed for business in black pumps, black hose, black skirt, black blazer and white shirt with notched collar and she was wearing her blonde hair up the way some office matrons do. But there was no disguising her youth. She reminded me of a little girl playing dress up. A very pretty little girl.

"Exactly how old are you?" I asked.

"I'll be eighteen in a couple of weeks," she answered without hesitation—I would have guessed younger. "Only please don't say you can't help me until you've heard why I've come."

Rachel's request came in a voice that made me guess others of my profession had already given her the bum's rush, as well they should—minors are not legally bound by contracts and working for them can be both ethically and financially dangerous. But I liked the way she came into my office alone; the way she met my eyes without turning away; the way she stood with feet apart and hands on her hips as if daring me to throw her out. You don't often see that kind of self-assurance in America's youth these days so I nodded my head, gestured toward the chair in front of my desk and told her to talk to me. Besides, she was cheerleader pretty and I was enough of a dirty old man to appreciate it...

The homicide cop gave me a knowing guffaw. Yeah, he knew my kind.

"I want you to investigate my stepfather," the girl told me.

That was different. Usually young women come to me for background checks on their boyfriends.

"Isn't love grand?" the homicide cop asked.

"You want to hear this story or don't you?"

"Sorry, sorry. Go on."

"Why?" I asked her. "Why investigate your stepfather?"

"He wants to adopt me," she said. "He wants me to take his name."

"Is that a bad thing?"

"Not necessarily," she admitted. "He loved my mom. At least he always treated her like he did. She died two months ago."

"I'm sorry," I told her.

"She had a brain tumor."

I winced at the thought of it. "I'm sorry," I repeated.

Rachel sighed and bowed her head like it was a subject she had lingered over too often for too long. I changed the subject.

"How does he treat you?" I asked.

"Like his most important asset," she answered, her head coming up. "My stepfather uses business terms in casual conversation. Mom was his partner.

Their marriage was a merger. And he said acquiring me was the best part of the deal."

She smiled briefly; I nearly missed it.

"Anyway," she continued. "After Mom's death, my stepfather said he wanted to adopt me; make it official; give me his name; make me his heir. He said he wanted to make sure I'd never have to worry about money or anything else. You probably know his name. Steven Palke? He was in the news just a couple of days ago."

Familiar, but I couldn't place it.

Rachel said, "Nine months ago Steven bought eighty percent of a computer software start-up that was on the verge of bankruptcy, a company that was trying to develop a more efficient browser for the Internet. Last week these guys in Washington—the state, not the city—bought the company AND the browser system for seventy million dollars; I think they want to keep it off the market. Steven earned fifty-six million on the deal and was hailed as this financial wizard."

I did some quick recapping: "Your stepfather loves you, treats you well, he's worth fifty-six million bucks and he wants you to become his heir. I don't see a problem here."

Rachel took a deep breath. She answered with the exhale.

"I was kidnapped nine months ago," she confided. "It wasn't in the papers; the police weren't notified; it happened during the Thanksgiving break so none of my friends or teachers knew I was missing..."

I started to take notes.

"A dark-colored van pulled up next to me while I was on my way home from school. A man wearing a black hood jumped out, grabbed me, pulled me inside. I screamed but I guess no one heard me. They blind-folded me, tied my arms and legs and drove to a house with an attached garage, a split-level way out in the suburbs with white tile in the kitchen and new carpet."

"How can you be sure?" I asked.

"They didn't do a good job with the blindfold," Rachel answered. "They left a crack at the bottom." She placed a finger a half inch below her eye to show me. "I could see what was beneath my feet."

"I meant that the house was in the suburbs."

Rachel hesitated, then answered, "We drove for an awfully long time. At least an hour."

"Okay," I said.

She took another deep breath.

"There were two of them," she continued. "A man and a woman. I think they were married because they called each other 'honey' and 'dear'— they never used proper names. They were very kind to me, believe it or not. They never threatened me; never said they were going to kill me or anything like that. Also—and this is where things get goofy—they always referred to my stepfather as MISTER Palke. It was Mr. Palke this and Mr. Palke that. One time the man was feeding me soup and the woman said, 'It's time to call Mr. Palke,' and the man said, 'Mr. Palke can wait' and the woman said..."

Rachel leaned forward on her chair so I would have no trouble hearing her.

"The woman said, 'We don't want to make him mad.' Do you believe that? They kidnap his stepdaughter but they don't want to make Mr. Palke angry?"

It didn't sound right to me, either.

"Anyway, what happened was the kidnappers demanded one million dollars in ransom and gave my stepfather forty-eight hours to raise it—I could hear them talking on the phone. Two days later the kidnappers got their million bucks and I was dropped off at Minnehaha Falls, near my home in Minneapolis."

"So your stepfather came up with the money," I assumed.

"No, sir," said Rachel. "He could only get half of it on such short notice. I found out later that the rest—five hundred thousand dollars—came from my father. My *real* father. You have to understand that at the time I was just thrilled to get home okay and then later my mom... Anyway, I didn't give much thought to any of this until I read the newspaper articles about Steven."

"What about them?" I asked.

"They pointed out that he earned the fifty-six million dollars on a five hundred thousand dollar investment—an investment he made only three days AFTER the kidnappers released me."

"And now you think that the kidnapping was a scam," I said, putting my highly-honed deductive abilities to the test. "You think that your stepfather staged the kidnapping to defraud your real father out of the five hundred thousand dollars that he later put into the computer company."

"I don't know," Rachel said. "I think so, but... Could you find out for me? For sure, I mean? Before I agree to be adopted? Steven has already changed his will and his lawyers are working on the adoption papers; he wants to file after my eighteenth birthday so my real father can't challenge it. But I don't want to be Steven's daughter if he's a thief and a kidnapper."

I was thinking that for fifty-six million bucks Saddam Hussein could adopt me. But then I'm old and cynical. Rachel was not and for a few moments I prayed that she never would be.

I cast aside all my reservations about working for the chronologically-challenged and did what later turned out to be a foolish thing.

I said, "Okay."

After hustling the girl out of my office, I turned to my notes. I was struck by how casual the kidnappers had seemed in Rachel's narration. They hadn't even bothered to use an outside phone. They were not afraid their calls would be traced; they were not afraid that they would be caught. This supported Rachel's suggestion that her stepfather might have arranged everything. And, I reasoned, he might have used a telephone to do it.

I had a hunch. If the kidnappers drove for an hour or more after they snatched Rachel, they not only might have driven outside the city, it's possible they had driven outside the local area code. If so, any calls Steven Palke made to them would be long-distance and listed on his telephone records.

I turned to my computer. I'm not hacker enough for major spoofs, but the telephone company is easy; the telephone company is about as secure as a box of corn flakes...

"Wait a minute," the homicide cop interrupted. "Are you telling me that you broke into the telephone company's computers!"

"Off the record, right?"

"Jesus Christ, Taylor," the cop muttered.

An hour later I was studying a laser print-out. The Palke's had made seventeen long-distance telephone calls from their home in the month of November—eight to a Cambridge, Minnesota number during the days leading up to and immediately following the kidnapping. Cambridge is an hour's drive north of the Twin Cities.

I punched the number.

"You've reached Don and Judy Strickland," a machine answered. "We can't come to the phone right now, but if you leave your name and number, we'll get back to you."

It took me ninety minutes to find the Stricklands' home using the phone book and an Itasca County map. I parked in the driveway. It was a split-level with attached garage—just as Rachel described— that had been built when they still put windows in garage doors. I peeked inside. There was not enough light to determine the exact color, but sure enough the garage contained a dark-looking van.

I walked around to the front door. I wasn't sure what I was going to say when the Stricklands answered my knock. "Are you the couple that Steven Palke hired to kidnap his stepdaughter?" Something like that. Only they didn't answer my knock or the low screaming of the doorbell. It was five-forty PM by my watch. Perhaps they hadn't yet arrived home from work, assuming they still lived there. I wouldn't if I had a million bucks. I tried the doorknob. It gave.

Something was terribly wrong. My heart didn't stop and my blood didn't suddenly run cold but I felt it just the same; felt it in a way that made me wish I was carrying a gun. I leaned on the front door and it swung inward slowly. A wave of cold air washed over me as I stepped across the threshold. The air conditioner was on high even though the weather was pleasant for Minnesota in August, seventy-five in the shade. I began to shiver.

I stepped into the living room. The carpet beneath my feet was new. So was most of the furniture; the place looked like it had been recently remodeled and refurnished. I called out.

"Hello! Anybody home?"

The kitchen was separated from the living room by a wide arch. I took three cautious steps toward it.

"Anybody home?" I called again.

I took another step, looked beyond the arch and got my answer.

What was left of Don and Judy Strickland was sprawled across the kitchen floor. Someone had torn their bodies apart with a sawed-off at close range.

A sound like rushing air filled my ears and muscles clenched in my neck, shoulders and legs. But I didn't panic. I closed my eyes and swallowed the air sound away; six or seven deep breaths quieted my heart and steadied my pulse rate. I had been a homicide cop in St. Paul and I knew how to do it, how to switch off my emotions and force myself into a kind of dispassionate mind set in which dead bodies become little more than props in a stage drama, a work in progress. Only I must have lost the knack during the four years since I pulled the pin because when I opened my eyes again the kitchen had become distorted: the walls and floor tile were now white light without borders, the splattered blood seemed to glow and the bodies shimmered like a heat mirage on an asphalt highway. I shielded my eyes with my hand. In the distance I heard a sound like a barking seal. It was me retching. I turned away and walked deep into the living room. I tried again to de-sensitize myself to my surroundings. It took a long time. I couldn't get past the image in my head that Don and Judy Strickland were holding hands when they died.

Eventually, I went back to the kitchen and lingered long enough to determine that Don and Judy were killed early that morning—the kitchen table set for breakfast and frozen waffles ready for the toaster gave it away. Next, I checked the doors. No forced entry. That could mean the Stricklands knew their killer. It could also mean that they opened the door to a stranger and the stranger forced them inside with the shotgun.

I found an office on the second floor. There was a file on top of the desk but its contents didn't interest me—only receipts from builders, carpet layers and furniture stores dated two weeks earlier. I began rifling drawers. That didn't help me, either. Impatiently, I looked up and around the room. Maybe the walls could give me a clue. To my astonishment, they did.

Framed in gold above the desk was a two-day-old article from the business section of Minneapolis-based *StarTribune* with the headline: "Local firm's browser wins big in world wide net war."

The article was accompanied by a photograph of a man sitting next to an elaborate computer system. Standing behind the man was a thirty-ish couple that looked exactly like the Stricklands except they weren't splattered with blood. The cutline read: "Facing bankruptcy just nine months ago, the firm owned by Donald and Judy Strickland and their benefactor, Minneapolis financier Steven Palke (sitting), was sold for seventy million yesterday." Six paragraphs in, the story included the date Palke made his five hundred thousand dollar investment—November 31, two working days after the kidnappers released Rachel. "Steven made it a wonderful Thanksgiving," said Judy Strickland.

I was in and out in fifteen minutes—fifteen long minutes—leaving nothing behind to place me at the scene; carrying away only another nightmare. I stopped at a convenience store on Highway 65 and called the Itasca County Sheriff's Department. I called direct instead of using 9-1-1 because I didn't want the conversation taped and reported that there was something terribly wrong at the Strickland home. They wanted more information, such as my name but I refused to give it. I didn't want to get involved. An hour later I arrived at the home Rachel Hartman shared with her stepfather.

It was an old house but not stately, big but not a mansion. Fifty-six million could buy about two hundred houses just like it in a community where you need an invitation to get past the gate.

Rachel answered the doorbell. She had changed from her black suit to a pair of white pleated shorts under a blue and white V-neck tee that somehow made her look older than she seemed in my office.

"What are you doing here?" she wanted to know. I pushed past her without answering.

"Is your stepfather home?" I asked.

"In the back..."

"Where?"

"Is there something wrong?"

I told her. She didn't take the news well. Her legs folded under her like an accordion and she collapsed at my feet.

"My father did it, my father did it," she repeated when I bent to pick her up.

That's what I was thinking, that Palke did the Stricklands to keep them quiet, although... Who were they going to talk to? And why? They made fourteen million off the deal. That's when Rachel told me about her father. Her REAL father. Abe 'The Cleaver' Hartman.

"Didn't you ask about him earlier when Rachel was in your office?" the homicide cop asked.

"No"

"Why not?"

"It didn't seem pertinent at the time."

The cop began to chuckle, leaving me with the distinct impression that he didn't think much of my investigative skills.

"Talk to my father," she begged.

"Me?" I asked her. "You talk to your father. He likes you. Me he might shoot. Or worse."

"That's nonsense," Rachel insisted.

"Know how he got the nickname 'The Cleaver?'" I asked her. "When Abe was still a young man, the mobs in Milwaukee and Kansas City tried to take over his business. Hartman chopped up the shooters they sent and used their body parts to mark his territory, scattering arms and legs and torsos around the perimeter of the Twin Cities."

Rachel closed her eyes and covered her mouth with her hand; her body shuddered like it was the first time she was told about her father and maybe it was. I instantly regretted telling the story. But then I got to thinking. She already suspected that her father murdered two people with a shotgun. What did I have to feel guilty about? I told her to call him herself.

"I will," Rachel promised. "I'll call him later. But first you must talk to him."

"And tell him what?"

"Tell him that Steven had nothing to do with the kidnapping. Tell him that it was the Stricklands, all of it."

"Think he'll believe me?"

Rachel thought for a moment.

"No," she said finally. "But he'll believe me when I tell him I don't want Steven harmed."

"Then tell him," I suggested.

She shook her head.

"My father believes in the code."

"What code?" I asked.

"The code, you know, about avenging wrongs done to your family and friends; about making sure people respect your family name..."

"You've been watching way too many movies, young lady," I told her. "There is no such code; there never has been."

"My father believes in it," Rachel insisted.

I told her I had my doubts.

"Mr. Taylor, if I ask my father not to harm Steven he'll have no choice," she said. "He'll have to say no because of the code. But if you tell him that Steven had nothing to do with the kidnapping and then I ask him, he'll say yes because then he'll have a choice. He can let Steven live and still save face. He won't believe me. But he loves me so he'll do it."

"You're deluding yourself," I told her.

"Please, Mr. Taylor," she begged. "It's the only way I can save my stepfather. Please. I'll pay you more money."

"I haven't spent the money you paid me this morning," I told her. And that, ultimately, was the reason why I agreed to her plan. Until the thousand ran out, Rachel was still the boss. Of course, I could have given back the money but that was unthinkable. You never give back the money. I

know PIs who would stop drinking in the same
saloons as I do if they heard I did such a thing.

*The cop shook his head at me like he was
disappointed.*

Abe Hartman began his criminal career while
still a child in the late 1920's. He was a newsie
working the lobby of the old Senator Hotel in
Minneapolis when the FBI offered him fifty cents a
week to note the comings and goings of the
gangsters who stayed there under assumed names.
Hartman promptly reported the arrangement to
Isadore "Kid Cann" Blumenfeld, the gangster who
controlled the "Minneapolis Combination." A
grateful Blumenfeld told Hartman to take the deal
and then paid him five bucks a week—a
Depression-era fortune—to confuse the feds with
false information that he supplied. It was the
beginning of a near father-son relationship that
lasted over three decades—Kid Cann even paid
Hartman's way to Princeton University.

After Blumenfeld was sent to federal prison for
white slavery in '61, Hartman took control of the
Combination, running it with Ivy League adroitness
and conservatism; always keeping a low profile,
staying away from the clubs and social functions
that Blumenfeld loved so much. The only time the
StarTribune printed his name was when he married
the daughter of a prominent Minneapolis banker
thirty-six years his junior. So successful was he in
fact, that when the feds used the RICO statutes to
bust him over a stock scam in '84, the local

population was astonished. Except for a few Asian gangs, it was convinced organized crime didn't exist in the Twin Cities.

All of this I knew. Rachel filled in the rest.

While Abe was doing his dime in federal prison, his wife divorced him and was granted sole custody of their daughter. Abe did not contest this. He was sixty-four with an uncertain future. The wife was twenty-eight, beautiful and rich—she married Palke not too long after. When Abe was released after serving two-thirds of his sentence, he tried to re-establish himself in Rachel's life, claiming that he was retired from crime. His ex-wife forbade visitation just the same and he was forced to watch his daughter grow up from afar. That frustration lasted until a rebellious Rachel turned thirteen years old and sought him out against her mother's wishes. They started visiting on the sly. Rachel's mother pretended to not know this, fearful that her protestations would only strengthen the bond between father and daughter. Instead she confined herself to the occasional personal attack, often referring to Abe as "that jailbird" in her daughter's presence. Yet it was Abe Hartman to whom she and her new husband turned to for help when Rachel was kidnapped, which made me think Mom might have been in on the scam, too.

I found Hartman's residence just off Glenwood Avenue near Theodore Wirth Park and at first I figured I had the wrong address. It was a modest house in a middle-class neighborhood that was largely built in the fifties and had been declining ever since. I had expected something considerably more opulent.

I knocked. The front door opened the length of a chain. Half a face peeked through the crack. "Yeah?" the face said.

I flashed my ID, announced, "I'm Holland Taylor. I'd like to speak to Mr. Hartman."

"Mr. Hartman speaks to nobody," the half face said and shut the door.

I knocked again. The door opened. "Get lost," half face told me this time. The door closed before I could speak.

I took a deep breath and knocked again. This time the door flew open. Half face became a handsome young man in his early twenties with brown hair, hazel eyes and a snarl. He grabbed the lapel of my jacket with his right hand and poked the index finger of his left hand into my face.

"Listen, jerk..."

Before he could say more, I grasped his right hand with my left and yanked down. At the same time I cupped his elbow with my right hand and pushed up. The pressure of the hold took him off his feet. I brought him down across the bottom of the door jam and applied even more pressure, touching the tip of his elbow against his jaw. The pain in his shoulder joint had to be excruciating but he refused to cry out.

"What's this?"

I turned toward the question without releasing my hold. Abe Hartman stood in the hallway clutching a copy of *People* magazine. He was wearing a dark blue suit that looked two sizes too big on him.

"I'm sorry, Mr. Hartman," the young man replied between clenched teeth. "He took me by surprise."

Hartman grimaced in a way that made me think it was the worst possible answer the young man could have given.

"I apologize for disturbing you, Mr. Hartman," I said politely—yeah, like I was going to be rude to The Cleaver. "My name is Holland Taylor. I'm a private investigator working for your daughter. She asked me to speak with you."

Hartman gestured toward the young man.

I released the hold. The young man sprang to his feet and closed the door. He did not rub his shoulder, although I knew he wanted to. Nor did he mad-dog me, give me one of those "I'll get you" looks much favored these days by young men who feel they've been dissed. Instead he looked directly at the old man and waited for instructions. He had discipline. I liked that.

Hartman moved into the living room without speaking. The young man gestured with his head to follow Hartman and I did. The young man followed me—not too close, but close enough. He'd definitely be someone to step aside from once he gained a little experience.

"This is Vern Miller," Hartman said, gesturing toward the young man. "No relation to the Verne Miller whom I had the pleasure of meeting many years ago, the man who machine gunned all those cops during the Kansas City Massacre in '33. This Vern is considerably more able."

I nodded—what do you say to an introduction like that?

Hartman settled into an over-stuffed chair as if he had spent a lot of time there. He gestured toward another chair across from him. I sat. Miller stood one pace behind and one pace to the right of me. His hands hung loosely at his side.

"I met Verne—the first Verne, not this one—in what? Must of been '28, '29," Hartman said. "I was just a boy then, running errands for Mr. Blumenfeld; met him at the Cotton Club in Minneapolis—that was one of Mr. Blumenfeld's joints."

Hartman sighed, pleased with the memory.

The Cleaver was not at all what I expected. I knew he was in his seventies, but he looked much older than that. His hair was wispy and white, his blue eyes watery. And he was underweight. His five-five frame carried maybe one hundred pounds; like his suit, his skin seemed too big for him. He spoke as if he had a cold. I had to remind myself that he was a stone killer.

"The Twin Cities, especially St. Paul, was wide open in those days," Hartman continued. "As long as you paid the cops on time and didn't commit any crimes within the city limits, a guy on the lam was welcome to stay: John Dillinger, Homer Van Meter, Ma Barker and her boys, Creepy Karpis, Machine Gun Kelly, Harvey Bailey, Leon Gleckman, Big Ed Morgan, Jelly Nash. I met them all working for Mr. Blumenfeld. I didn't meet Al Capone when he was here, but I shook hands with Bugsy Siegel. Nice man. He was in town to spring a couple of his boys from Stillwater but he couldn't manage it. You can bet those boys lived pretty good in prison, though.

"Verne Miller loved to play golf," Hartman said, segueing into another anecdote. "Most of the bank robbers of that era loved to swing the sticks, except Nash—Jelly thought it was the dumbest game in the world. The feds knew this, of course and they paid caddies and equipment managers to inform whenever the guys showed up for a round. That's how they got Bailey, Jimmy Keating and Tommy Holden. They caught them on the eighth hole at Mission Hills in Kansas City. They almost got Dillinger, too, right over here on the Keller Golf Course in Maplewood. On the third hole it was. But Johnny saw 'em coming and hopped a freight train that ran near the course, leaving his clubs behind..."

I glanced up at Miller. He was listening intently, his eyes glistening like a baseball fan listening to Ted Williams and Joe DiMaggio reminiscing about the '49 pennant race.

"Excuse me, Mr. Hartman," I said, real polite. Behind me Miller made a sound like a growl. "I'm sorry to interrupt, but I'm here on business."

"Yes, yes, of course," said Hartman. "My daughter."

"She asked me to speak with you on behalf of her stepfather."

Hartman snorted, spat the word "stepfather" like it was phlegm. The geniality he exhibited while discussing his mis-spent youth disappeared and suddenly there was no mistaking who Abe "The Cleaver" Hartman was.

"For fourteen years Rachel lived under his roof as a daughter and he does this!" Hartman said, his voice rising into a shout. "What kind of man kidnaps his own child?"

Hartman began to cough violently. He regained control long enough to say, "I'll kill the sonuvabitch." Then the coughing jag increased and he excused himself from the room. Miller made an effort to help but Hartman waved him away.

"How long?" I asked.

There was a deep sadness in Miller's eyes when he said, "A month, maybe two. The cancer is everywhere and the doctors can't help him."

A few moments passed and Hartman returned. He saw in my face that something had changed and looked accusingly at Miller.

"Don't blame him," I said. "It was an easy guess."

Hartman frowned slightly and settled into his chair.

"I was always afraid I'd get it like Dapper Dan Hogan in '28, blown up in my own car," he said. "Right now that doesn't sound like such a bad way to go."

I looked away. The man had been a criminal for seven decades yet I was sad he was dying. Sympathy for the devil. Or maybe it was for his daughter. My emotions became all tangled and I had to force myself to focus on the job at hand.

"Mr. Hartman, your daughter says Steven Palke had nothing to do with the kidnapping. She says she doesn't want you to kill him."

"Is that what she says?"

"Verbatim."

Hartman snorted. "We don't kill people," he insisted. "Isn't that right, Vern?"

"That's right," Miller said without conviction.

"As if you ever did," I added.

Hartman smiled, coughed into his hand.

"My day is past," he said after coming up for air. "By the time I was released from prison the combination was gone. Splintered apart; no way to piece it back together. Even if there was, I didn't have the energy. Or the resources. The feds used RICO to take almost everything. I had enough to live on, no more."

"You had enough to give Steven Palke five hundred thousand dollars in cash," I reminded him.

"I didn't..." Hartman stopped like he remembered something and chuckled; the chuckle brought on another coughing fit. "I didn't say I was destitute," he said when he recovered. "But that money was all I could raise; all I had left."

I glanced around the living room. It reminded me of the declining neighborhood in which Hartman lived. I believed him when he said he was broke; I was surprised he had enough for his share of the ransom.

"Your daughter said she would call you," I told him.

Hartman smiled.

"It's always a pleasure to hear from Rachel," he said. "We don't see her nearly enough, do we, Vern?"

Miller shook his head.

And I went home.

"Just like that?" the homicide cop asked.

"Just like that."

"It didn't occur to you to warn Palke that his life was in danger?"

"I did warn him. Didn't I tell you?"

"You missed that part," the cop said.

"When I was here the first time. I told Palke that the Stricklands had been murdered, that Abe Hartman probably arranged it and that Hartman was probably after him, too."

"What did he say?"

"He told me I was mistaken. He said he couldn't imagine that Abe Hartman had anything against him or the Stricklands. I told him to have it his own way and went to see Abe."

An hour later Rachel called. She spoke breathlessly, her voice pleading. "I need you. Please come." I went.

I reached her home in fifteen minutes, driving at speeds that invited arrest. The sun had set by the time I pulled in at the curb. There were lights on in the house but I could see no one through the windows. Vern Miller was seated on the concrete steps leading to the front door. I was walking toward him when I heard the scream: loud, piercing, a female sound of great anguish.

Miller was up and through the door. I ran toward it. I had just reached the steps when I heard another scream, this one even louder. It was followed by the multiple, sharp "cracks" of a semi-automatic handgun, something heavy—three shots fired. Almost immediately a single, hollow explosion responded. Shotgun. Another scream. Then another. I was through the door, down the hall and into the living room before it faded into a low, aching moan. I found Rachel Hartman kneeling there, cradling the head of her step-father on her lap; her arms and clothes were drenched with blood. The Glock was on the floor next to them. Across the room Vern Miller held the body of Abe Hartman close to his chest. A sawed-off Mossberg pump was nearby. Rachel was pleading with her step-father, "Don't die, don't die." Miller didn't say a word to his employer. He wouldn't have heard anyway. Both Palke and Hartman were dead. Take my word for it.

"The Hennepin County Attorney's gonna love this," the homicide cop sighed. "Old-time mobster and nouveau-riche financier slaughter each other for love of the daughter they both shared. Forget the local guys, this is the kind of thing that goes national. 20-20 might even pick it up. Just what I need."

He was pissed and I didn't blame him. Nobody wants the media looking over their shoulder while they work.

"At least it looks open and shut," he added.

"Think so?" I asked him.

He stared at me for a good six beats before answering: "Let's see if your story matches what the kids have to say."

Neither of us was surprised that it did.

Rachel buried Abe "The Cleaver" Hartman in Calvary Cemetery on the north side of St. Paul because that's where Dapper Dan Hogan was buried and that's the way Hartman wanted it. Only there were hundreds of mourners to bid adieu to the man who first organized crime in St. Paul and just a handful to salute Hartman. Like he said, his time had passed. Even the media had lost interest; a single camera crew shot the funeral and it departed before the finish.

Three people lingered at the grave after the rabbi muttered the final good-bye: Rachel Hartman, Vern Miller, me. Miller was the first to leave. Rachel smiled weakly and thanked me for coming; she said it was thoughtful. I cut that off right away.

"I don't like being used," I told her.

"I don't understand," she said but I knew she did.

"It looks like the Hennepin County Attorney bought your story," I told her.

She smiled slightly and looked off toward where Vern Miller was waiting next to a black limousine.

"You mean our story, don't you?"

"Yeah, I mean our story," I told her. "Did I tell it right; just the way you wanted me to?"

The smile never left her face but there was an edge to it now.

"I have no complaints," she said.

"There's a hole in it, you know. A big one."

"Is there?" she asked, real coy.

"Big enough so the rest just won't fit."

"What?"

"You told me the Stricklands' had new carpeting, new tile in their kitchen..."

"And so they did," Rachel said.

"Yes, but it was new two weeks ago, not last November when you claimed they kidnapped you," I told her. "I saw the receipts."

Rachel closed her eyes, smiled slightly, opened them again.

"My mistake," she said calmly.

"You hadn't been to the Stricklands' home until you went there to kill them," I added. "There was no kidnapping."

"You can't prove that," she told me.

"Palke struck it seriously rich and made you his heir," I continued. "But that didn't satisfy you. Like a lot of kids today you want it all and right now. So you invented the kidnapping..."

"Mr. Taylor, you make me sound so... calculating," Rachel interrupted, enjoying the sound of her own voice.

"You killed the Stricklands. Why? Because in your story, your step-father required accomplices and who better than the business partners who would directly benefit from the alleged kidnapping. As for Abe... He had been out of it for a long time but his reputation lived on. You were counting on that. Who would doubt that Abe 'The Cleaver"

Hartman would kill the people who kidnapped his daughter? Not me.

"So, you coerced Abe to your house; you had Vern wait outside while he and your step-father spoke privately. Then you waited for me to arrive, the white knight riding to aid the damsel in distress..."

"Nice metaphor," Rachel interrupted again.

"When you saw me arrive, you shot your father with Palke's gun then killed Palke with the shotgun. I rushed in and found you cradling Palke's body. Course, at the time I didn't realize you only wanted to stain yourself with blood so the cops couldn't prove you fired the guns.

"And me? I was merely the narrator, the disinterested third party who put all the pieces together for the cops: you were kidnapped, Abe killed the kidnappers outta revenge, getting himself killed in the process. You have to admit, I made a helluva corroborating witness."

"You earned your money," Rachel agreed.

"How much to do you stand to inherit? Fifty-six million?"

"Closer to sixty-five," Rachel said. "So what happens now? Blackmail?"

I told her: "You confess to the cops. Confess or I'll rat you out."

"To who?" she wanted to know. "With what evidence?"

I gestured toward where Vern Miller stood next to a black limousine. "The code, remember? Miller won't like it that you murdered his friend and

29

mentor. He might decide to do something about it."

"Think so?" she asked softly. And then louder, "Vern, could we have a moment, please?"

He walked toward us.

"Vern," Rachel said when he was within earshot. "Mr. Taylor says if I don't confess my crimes to the police department, he's going to tell you all about them. I assume he expects you to punish me."

Miller smiled broadly.

"And I will, too," he said. "As soon as I get you home."

"Promise?" she asked.

"You're in it together?" I asked. "The two of you?"

"The three of us," admitted Miller.

"Abe?"

"Mr. Hartman had nothing but hard dying to look forward to," Miller said. "He wasn't happy about that..."

"And he wasn't happy that the business he and Isadore Blumenfeld had spent their lifetimes building had disappeared while he was in prison," Rachel added.

"He set it up so we would have the resources to rebuild the combination," Miller said.

"It was his plan," Rachel said. "One last great heist. The perfect crime."

"He went out on top," Miller concluded.

"Yeah, with you carrying him on your shoulders," I said.

"It was his plan!" spat Rachel, outraged. "Don't you dare take that away from him. We helped, sure. He was too weak to get around. We had to shoot the Stricklands for him and in the end, I had to shoot my step-father; Abe couldn't hold the gun steady. But it was his idea; his plan."

"Yeah, I figured that all along," I said. "I just wanted to hear you say it."

"What?"

"I knew he was in on it," I confessed. "He claimed he kicked in half a million for the ransom; he didn't have it. And you two..."

"What?" Rachel repeated.

"You two don't have the wit for this kind of caper."

"What are you talking about?"

"Too young. Too inexperienced."

Miller smiled. "Maybe so," he said. "But we have fifty-six million dollars."

"Sixty-five," Rachel corrected him. "And there's absolutely nothing you can do about it," she told me.

"Oh, I wouldn't say that."

"Yeah? What are you going to do?" Miller wanted to know, clenching his fists like he wanted to pop me one.

I reached inside me shirt and removed the microphone that was taped just below my rib cage. I held it for them to see.

"I'm going to testify at your trial," I told them.

A moment later, a swarm of police officers led by the Minneapolis homicide cop crossed the cemetery to take them.

* * *

"*A guy like Abe spends a lifetime learning how to act, what to do when push comes to shove,*" I told the homicide cop later. "*But kids today, they don't know how to behave and they refuse to take the time to learn.*"

"*I hear that,*" the cop replied.

"*They don't even know enough to keep their mouths shut. Think Abe would have spoken so freely about murder?*"

"*Not in this lifetime,*" the cop agreed.

"*Kids,*" I said contemptuously.

"*Yeah, kids.*"

Author's Note: I had the great pleasure of teaching a writing seminar with the marvelous Tami Hoag a few years back at the legendary Once Upon A Crime Mystery Bookstore in Minneapolis. Tami, of course, is best known for writing crackerjack thrillers. She started her career, though, as a romance novelist. I made the obnoxious comment that "Any moron can write a romance"—yes, alcohol was involved. Tami disagreed, quite vehemently, as I recall. So I wrote a story and sold it to True Romance Magazine *which printed it under the title* "How To Trick A Woman Into Having Sex." *The editor liked it so much she called and asked for more stories because mine "was like real literature." I took a copy of the magazine to Tami the next time she was in town. She looked at it and said, "I guess you're right. Any moron can write a romance."*

The Sultan of Seduction

The self-proclaimed Sultan of Seduction bounced into the hotel conference room and mounted the low stage to thunderous applause—or at least as much thunder as thirty white guys could manage. He pumped his fist, hopped up and down and raised his arms in triumph while his audience danced with him. The ovation lasted a full minute, with "The Believers," as the guys labeled themselves, chanting "Sultan, Sultan." Toward the end of it, the Sultan winked at me and smiled as if to say, "See, I told you so."

I shrugged in reply. Maybe if I hadn't seen the hotel's blonde desk clerk blow him off just minutes before, I might have been more impressed. I wondered how The Believers would take it if I told them the truth about their guru. Coming from the only woman in the room, they probably wouldn't believe it. I was the enemy, after all, and that's what the seminar was all about—defeating the enemy.

Still, it wasn't my job to sully the Sultan's reputation. I was there to keep him alive.

I had met the Sultan at the Minneapolis-St. Paul International Airport and was surprised by his appearance: lanky and without muscle tone, thin face, sallow complexion, short and prematurely gray hair, thick black-rimmed glasses, white button-down cotton shirt, black polyester slacks, white socks and black wingtips. Not exactly the "babe-magnet" that had been described to me.

"You were expecting a movie star?" he asked.

"Something like that."

"That's the whole point," he claimed. "The Believers see me and they know that if I can seduce women, they can, too."

I didn't say a word, but my expression must have told him something. The Sultan glared at me.

"Wait here," he said, and went off to prove himself, accosting the attendant who had worked his flight, stopping her as she rolled her suitcase toward a shuttle bus.

At first, she seemed uncomfortable, yet she visibly relaxed as he spoke softly to her, wonderfully pleasant and sincere as he gazed into her green eyes. She was listening quite intently to everything he had to say, and I began to think, *Hmm, maybe he is a babe magnet,* right up until she balled her fist and whacked him on the chin. She would have bashed him again, but he looked so pathetic with his head tucked beneath crossed arms that she gave it up and moved on.

"You're supposed to protect me," he wailed when I reached his side.

"Next time I'll shoot."

I hustled the Sultan to my car and we proceeded to follow his agent's carefully crafted itinerary. First, he would have interviews at a couple of Twin Cities' radio stations, followed by two newspapers and a magazine. However, to the Sultan's chagrin, not one of the Cities' seven TV stations would put him on the air.

It was the agent's idea that a female private investigator be assigned to protect his client from evil feminists. He said there was poetry in it. *Yeah,* I thought. *Like the kind you read on bathroom walls.*

I begged the boss not to assign me. I told him it wasn't a bodyguard job anyway; more like chauffer for the day. But he pointed out that I was his only female operative and besides, the customer is always right. Personally, I think he considered the assignment to be just one big practical joke on me and I vowed to get even.

On I-35W heading north into downtown Minneapolis, the Sultan asked, "You're a private eye?" as if he couldn't believe it.

"Yep."

"Ever shoot anyone?"

"Not recently."

"You have nice legs."

"So I've been told."

"Nice body, too."

"I never get involved with clients," I announced, cutting him off at the pass.

"If I looked like a soap opera actor, I'll bet you would."

I didn't reply, keeping my eyes on the road.

"'Give me ten minutes to talk away my ugly face and I will bed the Queen of France.' Know who said that?"

"Voltaire."

He muttered a word rarely printed in the better magazines and turned away. I smiled. It's like my mom always said: "If you hide your intelligence so boys will like you, you'll find that the only boys who like you are stupid."

Most of the people who interviewed the Sultan did so with a straight face, even when he spoke of a conspiracy of "hysterical feminists" who would stop at nothing—including murder—to silence him. As proof that his life was in danger, he produced a letter threatening bodily harm if he should return to the Land of 10,000 Lakes.

I read it over his shoulder: *Stay away from Minnesota. You've done enough damage here.* It was printed in block letters with red ink on a single sheet of typing paper. It was unsigned.

The bad boys at one of rock stations wondered aloud if the letter was nothing more than a publicity ploy. The Sultan insisted it was authentic and that he was frightened; that's why his agent hired a bodyguard—albeit a female—to protect him during the duration of his stay.

The bad boys wouldn't let it go, however, and asked me on the air, "Does anyone *really* want to kill the Sultan?"

"You mean besides me?"

The Sultan didn't like my answer and during the commercial break, he told me so at decibels just below that of a 747. For four hundred bucks a day plus expenses, he felt he deserved better and he was right. But it was hard to take a man seriously who was pushing a book called *Scoring for Putzes.*

The Sultan of Seduction was in the sex business. Specifically, he sold, at exorbitant prices, books, ebooks, CDs, DVDs and admission to seminars that taught homely men how to get beautiful women onto bed—guaranteed. His first book, *How To Trick Any Woman You Want into Having Sex,* was a Top 25 on Amazon and his second babe-getting tutorial, *Scoring,* was moving up fast.

"I give men power and choice," he proclaimed proudly. "Before, a man might be in a crummy relationship with some over-weight dog because he couldn't get anyone better. But with my technique, he can dump his partner and move up. Even a regular guy can shag the most beautiful, most desirable women. He doesn't have to settle for second best.

"That's why the feminists are threatening my life," he added. "Because I'm disrupting the status quo."

The reporter for one of the newspapers compared the Sultan to William Hartman. It was Hartman, the reporter noted, who wandered the streets of Manhattan with a tape recorder in 1970 asking attractive women what it would take for a guy like him to score with a woman like her. He printed the answers in a book, *How To Pick Up Girls,* and made a fortune.

The Sultan bristled at the comparison.

"I'm light-years ahead of Harman," he insisted. "Have you read his book? Do you know what it says? It says if you want to pick up women just talk to them. Talk to them? Learn what they're about? Get real! I'm not dissing Hartman, okay? The man was a pioneer; you gotta recognize that. But he was only interested in *meeting* women and *dating* them. I don't care about that. Men today don't care about that. They want to know how to get women in bed with the least amount of effort. That's what I teach 'em."

What the Sultan taught his disciples was actually a little-known discipline called neurolinguistic programming. By the seventh time I heard him explain it, I had it down pat.

Neurolinguistic programming was developed in the early '70s by a couple of professors specializing in linguistics and theoretical psychology. They hit upon the radical notion that conventional therapy was unnecessary, that emotionally disturbed patients didn't need to work through past traumas to become healed. Instead, the professors argued that through an artful use of language, all those terrible "subjective human experiences" that ruin people's lives could be quickly and easily transformed in the unconscious mind into something less painful and less important.

Basically, they settle patients into a very light, conversationally induced hypnotic trance and, using hypnotic language patterns and embedded commands, convince them that the traumatic experiences that haunt their dreams really aren't so bad, after all.

Of course, it wasn't long before the more entrepreneurially inclined among us—used car salesmen come to mind—saw neurolinguistic programming as a tool of persuasion, as a means of selling just about anything to anyone—even the notion that men without looks, personality, charm, intelligence, money or power would be able to have sex with any woman they wanted.

"You hypnotize them," I said over dinner at a restaurant where I was sure no one would know me. "You hypnotize women into thinking you're some kind of stud-muffin instead of a loser."

"I'm not a loser. Bitch."

"Don't call me names. I'm the one carrying a gun, remember? And if you're not a loser, why do you need to hypnotize women to get them into bed?"

He didn't answer.

"A bit unethical, don't you think?" I said.

"I have tens of thousands of students around the world who don't think so."

"And how much money do you make off each?"

"It's not about money."

"What then?"

He set his fork carefully across his plate and looked at me as if he was about to say something profound.

"I didn't get laid until I was twenty-three and when I did, the girl was drunk," he said.

I had to ponder that for a moment, surprised by the conclusion I reached.

"Payback?" I said. "You're doing all this because you didn't have sex when you were a teenager?"

His eyes flared at me.

"Women like you, who look like you do, you're the kind that torment men, aren't you?" he said. "Men see you and know they can't have you. I bet you were the most popular girl in school—teasing the football heroes and basketball stars who lined up to spend their money on you. Other girls wanted to be just like you..."

I shook my head. That was someone else's experience.

"You never gave a thought to people like me, I bet," the Sultan said. "Never even glanced at anyone who didn't have good looks or money or a nice car."

In my mind, I flashed back to my high school heartthrob, the cute but geeky president of the chess club who drove a battered Ford, but I kept the memory to myself.

I said, "So to get revenge, now you claim to be this big-time seducer of women. You claim you can teach any man how to get any woman anytime."

"I'm not claiming anything. My program works." He glanced around the restaurant as he spoke. "It's about word patterns. It's about using words to capture and lead the imagination of your target. A guy can get oral sex from a complete stranger just by saying the right words at the right time, by making certain suggestions."

Only there was much more to it than that and he proceeded to show me, watching my eyes as he spoke, changing the tone of his voice, matching his body language to mine. I could feel him breathing at the same pace as I was. And although he was doing nearly all the talking, it was as if he had vanished and I was sitting there listening to the sounds in my own head.

It wasn't until a thin smile played over his lips that I realized what the Sultan was doing.

"Hey," I shouted.

He laughed.

"Still don't believe me?" he asked.

Out of the corner of his eye, he spied a woman as she moved to the bar. She was in her early twenties, blonde hair cascading over her shoulders. Her black skirt slid upward as she squirmed onto the stool, revealing a glimpse of her upper thigh. She pulled down the hem as she settled into place.

"Oh, yeah, bogey at two o'clock," the Sultan whispered gleefully. He made the sound of a World War II air raid siren as he slid out of the booth. "Watch and learn."

He sauntered confidently to the blonde's side. It was like the situation in the airport. The young woman's defense mechanisms went on alert, but slowly lowered as he spoke to her. I couldn't hear what he was saying, yet his words had a profound effect on the woman. She smiled dreamily and a look of bliss came over her face.

The Sultan leaned in close, still talking. The woman's eyes widened, her lips parted, she seemed to be remembering something that filled her with joy. The Sultan's eyes never wavered from hers. He continued to speak. The woman's cheeks flushed and her entire body trembled. Her hand moved to her crotch and she squeezed herself through the material of her skirt. A look that could only be described as amazement crept over her face.

The Sultan laughed at her. He turned his back on the woman and walked back toward me, chuckling loudly.

"See," he said.

I watched the woman over his shoulder. The look of amazement on her face was quickly replaced by one of bewilderment and then shame. She spun on her stool toward the bar, her face in her hands. She was shaking; she couldn't possibly understand what had just been done to her. A moment later, she ran past, heading for the door. Tears streaked her cheeks.

"Bastard."

The Sultan seemed surprised by my reaction.

"What?" he asked. "You're upset because of that bitch? How many guys has she screwed over, I wonder. How many guys did she make feel like dirt because she wouldn't talk to them, go out with them; give them the time of day? Huh? She got what she deserved."

I had nothing more to say to him. For a moment I hoped someone really was trying to kill him.

The Sultan was on a roll now. All the way to the evening seminar, he kept cracking sexist jokes at the rate of about fifteen a mile, laughing loudly until we hit the parking lot. We made our way through the lobby doors. He spied the desk clerk.

"Bogey at twelve o'clock high," he said and started doing the siren thing again.

The clerk greeted him openly; he was a guest after all. The Sultan leaned in and started speaking earnestly. A quizzical expression appeared on the woman's face. And after listening to his patter for a moment, she began to laugh. The Sultan wasn't laughing, though. For some reason, his sense of humor, such as it was, disappeared. He retreated hastily from the desk, the clerk's laughter stabbing at his back.

"Hey," she called to him. "If you're so hard up, why don't you just order Pay-For-View and jerk yourself a soda."

But that was then. Now he was basking in the adoration of The Believers, savoring their applause.

When it finally subsided, he asked, "So, are you guys getting any?"

The applause erupted again. At least a dozen of The Believers had stories to tell and the Sultan wanted to hear them; he wanted to add to the collection he posted on his website.

The room was far too big for the size of the crowd. Rows of chairs set in front of the low stage—most of them empty—had been divided into two sections with an aisle running between them. I found a seat in the back corner opposite the front door. It allowed me to take in the entire room with just turn of my head.

A black leather bag with a thick strap hung from my shoulder. Inside the bag was a Beretta Model 85 .380 double-action semi-automatic handgun. I made sure it was close to my hand. I was still convinced that there was no danger, that I had been hired merely as a prop to flash in front of the media. But I was a professional and I chose to act like one—especially among these screaming post-adolescents.

Most of the seminar participants were in the eighteen to twenty-four demographic group, the one most desired by advertisers for its lack of discretion in making impulse buying decisions, although there were more than a few in their thirties. Some of them glanced at me nervously; others with greedy smirks pasted on their faces. One man sitting in the back row didn't fit the demographic at all. I figured him for mid-fifties. He looked like someone's father.

He was wearing a workman's zipper jacket with the logo of the AFL-CIO stitched on the shoulder. He sat with his arms folded across his chest. He didn't cheer or applaud. If anything, he seemed bored, his head down, his eyes locked on the back of the chair in front of him. His right hand was pressed against the side of the jacket.

The Believers were telling their stories. One described how he shagged a hard-body at a coffeehouse just off the St. Paul campus of the University of Minnesota. He had taken her in the backseat of her car parked just down the street from a church. That led to another success story from a guy who claimed he played under the skirt of a coed on a bench just outside a church after talking to her for less than five minutes.

The mention of a church brought the workman's head up. He leaned forward, his hand on his knee. With his other hand, he unzipped the jacket.

Now it was the Sultan's turn.

"The last time I was in Minneapolis, I slushed a twenty-year-old *inside* a church," he said.

The rowdy crowd cheered, then quickly quieted as the Sultan continued. The workman was sitting straight up in his chair now, his head turned so that his left ear was tilted toward the speaker.

"It was the big church off, what's the name of the street, Milton?" the Sultan said.

"Yeah, Milton Avenue," someone shouted. "Near the movie theater."

"This woman was a real tease, sitting in a pew toward the back," the Sultan said. "She wasn't kneeling or praying, just sitting there looking straight ahead. The place was empty. I moved next to her, started to work on her..."

The workman rose up higher. He was only half-sitting on his chair, straining to hear.

"She had a beautiful mouth, very sensuous," the Sultan said. "So, you know I just had to run the BJ pattern on her."

The Believers applauded. The workman was on his feet.

"I had her eating imaginary chocolate-covered cherries out of my hand," the Sultan said. "Had 'em exploding in her mouth..."

The workman reached under his jacket. I eased the .380 out of my bag, holding it against the black leather, the safety off. I moved along the edge of the chairs, watching his hands—I always watch the hands. I was about eight feet away from the workman when he pulled out a white cloth from under his jacket.

My hands came up, my feet spread. I was in a Weaver stance, ready to shoot the workman in the center of his chest.

He brought the cloth to his nose and blew hard.

I lowered the gun and quickly shoved it back into the bag. A quick glance told me that no one had witnessed my mistake. The Believers were all too busy hanging onto each and every word that spilled from the Sultan's mouth.

I took a step backward. The workman glanced up at me and shook his head sadly.

"You believe this shit?" he asked.

I thumbed the safety of the Beretta into place and removed my empty hand from the bag.

"Did a ventilation job for the hotel," the workman said. "Guy gave me a ticket, said I should check out this Sultan guy. Only there ain't nothin' here but talk, you know? Guy tryin' to make you think he's somethin' with the ladies. Same B.S. I heard on the street corner when I was a kid; when I was in the army. Only this one, he's gotta bring the church into it. Fuck 'im."

When the workman left, I nearly went with him. But a job was a job and the Sultan was just getting warmed up.

He moved into the meat of the seminar, giving some background on the professors in California and their theories and explaining what it all meant for regular Joes like them—and the products he had for sale that would give them the power over women that they craved. A microphone was set up in the aisle between the chairs and The Believers lined up to ask questions. The line moved slowly.

Finally, a young man reached the mic. He could have passed for sixteen and maybe he was. Everything he was wearing—slacks, shirt and tie, sports jacket—seemed too big for him.

"I'd like to talk about the morality of all this," he said.

His remarks brought hoots from some of The Believers, yet a surprising number nodded their heads as if it was something they wished they had said. The Sultan waved him off before he could continue. He had heard it before and he had a ready answer.

"When we put a woman into a neurolinguistic trance and run patterns on her, we're opening her up to suggestions. But we're not forcing her to do anything against her will. We're only getting from her what she would probably give to someone else who had the looks and money and other advantages that we lack."

The boy would not be dismissed, though.

"That girl in the church," he said. "You took her into the vestibule and had her kneel in front of you…"

"Was she consenting?" the Sultan asked. "If she was, I don't see what the ethical question is."

"You play with a woman's emotions so she will do things that, under normal circumstances, she wouldn't do."

"Oh, she'd do them. Only not with us, right?"

"Right," many of The Believers answered.

"But would she?" the young man asked. "The girl in the church, why was she there? It wasn't to get picked up, was it? It's not like she was hanging out in a bar…"

"I think it's time to move on," the Sultan said.

"No. Listen to me." The young man's sudden outburst silenced The Believers. Even the Sultan stopped to listen from his perched on the low stage.

"Maybe she wasn't at the church to meet guys," he said. "Maybe she was there because she had lost a guy. Maybe that was the church where she would have been married if her fiancé hadn't been killed in a car accident one week before the wedding. Maybe she was lonely and hurt and confused and depressed to the point where suicide was an option and she didn't know what to do.

"Then you come along, acting so sincere and caring. Maybe she thought you actually were sincere and caring. Maybe you convinced her that she had found someone to fill the hole in her aching heart. And then you run your patterns on her, and in her vulnerability, she succumbs. And then you say, 'I'm finished with you, get lost.' And maybe in her horror and humiliation at what she had done and her betrayal—in church—of her one true love, she ends her life. And you—you brag about it."

I could see from the expression on the faces of many of The Believers, the kid had struck a nerve. Yet most of the guys were smirking; waiting for their guru's reply.

"That reminds me of a story," the Sultan said. "A girl calls a guy and says, 'Remember me? We met at a party two months ago and you said I was a good sport. Well, I'm pregnant with your child and I'm going to jump off the Lake Street Bridge.' And the guy says, 'My, you are a good sport.'"

The Believers broke into laughter and applause.

That's when the kid pulled the wheel gun.

The first shot froze us all into silence. The second had us diving for cover. The next four brought screams and a mad dash for the exits. I rolled to my knees while I fumbled for the Beretta. I brought it up, set the sights on the kid and realized in the split second before I squeezed the trigger that he was a she—and that the hammer was now falling on empty chambers.

"Drop the gun, drop it." I was screaming at her, attempting to startle her into compliance. She looked at me as if I had barely whispered.

"Drop the gun."

"Okay," she said.

The gun slipped from her fingers and fell on the carpet at her feet.

"Step back."

She stepped back.

I scooped up the gun and dropped it into my bag. It was only then that I looked for the Sultan. He was curled into a fetal position on the low stage and whimpering. I called his name, yet he did not respond.

"Are you hurt?" I asked.

His reply came in a whine. "No."

"Are you sure?"

"Uh huh."

Six shots at close range and the young woman had missed him. Goes to show, it's not as easy as it looks on TV.

I was still pointing the Beretta at her. I noticed for the first time that the large room was empty except for us.

"Who are you?" I asked.

"I'm not telling."

"What's your name?"

She shook her head.

"What are you doing here?"

She pointed at the Sultan, still rolled into a ball and weeping.

"I told him what would happen if he came back," she said.

"What you said about the woman in the church—was that true?"

"My big sister."

I glanced down at the Sultan. To say I was disgusted with him would have been too lenient.

"Are you going to shoot me?" the young woman asked.

"I doubt it." I lowered the Beretta.

"He's loathsome," she said.

"I can see how you might think that."

"I wish I had killed him."

"I'm glad you didn't. Otherwise, I wouldn't be able to let you go."

"What?"

"Quickly now, before the cops come. Go out that door." I pointed to the exit in the back of the room. "Hang a left in the corridor and keep going until you see a set of emergency doors. Hit 'em hard and keep running. Don't stop. And don't look back. Go now."

"Why…"

"Now."

She went.

I waited until I heard the whooping sound the emergency doors made when they were opened before I bent to the Sultan.

"Hey, there, big fella," I said. "It's all right now."

"Where's the man, the man with the gun?"

"It was a woman."

"A woman?"

"A hysterical feminist. She got away."

"A woman?" he repeated.

"Hell hath no fury, sir," I told him. "Hell hath no fury."

Author's Note: Calling themselves the Minnesota Crime Wave, some friends of mine named William Kent Krueger, Ellen Hart, Deborah Woodworth and Carl Brookins, decided to publish an anthology of mysteries, all of them written by Minnesota authors. They asked that I contribute a piece and I said, "Sure." But there were two strings attached. String one—the story had to incorporate at least four of eight clues provided by the editors: a headless Barbie doll, a page torn from a dictionary, footprints in snow, the sound of a train whistle, a temporary tattoo, the scent Obsession, a wig, a soiled ballet slipper. String two—the story had to take place in Fertile, Minnesota, about ten miles from the village of Climax. Apparently, the Wave was impressed by a newspaper headline that they teach to JO students here, an example of what not to do: Fertile woman killed in Climax. *So I drove to Fertile, a mere two hundred ninety mile jaunt from my house, spent the day doing research, then came home. I mentioned the trip to the Wave and told them I didn't think they could get that many good stories from a town with a population of eight hundred fifty. "Oh, yeah," Krueger told me. "We decided not to do that. Didn't we tell you?" No, no you didn't. But at least I got a decent story for my trouble. The* St. Paul Pioneer Press *wrote:* Housewright's 'A Domestic Matter,' about a guy who helps friends, has such a perfect O. Henry ending you want to reread it to figure out how he did it."

A Domestic Matter

I answered the phone at my desk in the city room of the Minneapolis *Star Tribune*.

"I'm in trouble," Jack said. He didn't bother to say "hello" or to identify himself, but then it wasn't necessary. We grew up together, went to school together, played on the same hockey teams since we were pee wees—it might have been a month since I spoke to him last, yet he could've just stepped outside for a smoke for all the difference it made.

"What now?" I said.

"My wife wants to kill me."

"Tell her if she needs any help to give me a call."

"I mean it, Danny…" He was one of the few people who still called me that. To everyone else I was Dan or Daniel or Thorn or to the occasional bartender, Mr. Thorn. "She wants me dead."

"Why should she be any different than the rest of us?"

"Dammit, Danny, I'm not kidding. Do I sound like I'm kidding? Tess is going to kill me."

"Why?"

"Because she found out I've been cheating on her."

"Oops."

"She found out and now she's, she's—you can tell just by looking at her that she wants to rip my heart out."

"Jeezuz, Jack. You've been married for fifteen years. How did you think she'd feel?"

"You know the way she's been. When you came up for the holidays, Tess could barely stand to be in the same room with either of us, always finding an excuse to be somewhere else."

"Don't remind me."

"Well, nothing's changed. We don't talk, we don't have sex—the love is gone, Danny."

"And you decided to cheat on her."

"I didn't decide to cheat. It's just—I met this girl. This woman. I was jogging and she was jogging and how many people do you know up here in

Fertile, Minnesota, who go jogging? Especially in the winter."

"You're the last of a dying breed."

"We don't even have sex that often. Mostly we just talk. We talk about everything. We talk about the things that Tess and I used to talk about."

"I'm sure that's a lot of comfort to your wife."

"She wants to kill me."

"Hell, Jack. I want to kill you."

"Danny, you're not listening. Tess took out a half million dollar insurance policy on my life without telling me. She gets another hundred fifty thousand if I'm murdered."

"Are you serious?"

"Hell, yes, I'm serious. What do you think I've been trying to tell you?"

I pulled out a tan-covered Reporter's Notebook. This wasn't a story I intended to write, but I had learned long ago—take lots of notes.

"Tell me everything, Jack. From the beginning."

Three days and a lot of frantic long distance calls later, I was in Fertile, Minnesota, population eight hundred eighty-seven, home of the Fertile-Beltrami Falcons. You can find it about two hundred seventy-five miles northwest of the Twin Cities on Highway 32, which came as a surprise to me. Until a couple of years ago, I didn't know you could take Highway 32 to the ends of the Earth. I learned different when I helped Jack and Tess move. She was a hospital administrator and Bridges Medical, a forty-nine bed facility just down the road in Ada, needed someone to run the place. He was a day-trader and figured he could earn a living anywhere he could plug in his PC.

It was late March. Light snow had just begun to fall when I pulled off the main drag and parked in front of Eats 'N' Antiques on Mill Street. I told the woman who ran the place that instead of the curios she displayed in her glass counters, I had come for a cup of joe and a slice of blueberry pie which my good friend Jack Edelson said was the very best in Minnesota.

The woman actually blushed, something you don't often see these days, and said, "That Mr. Edelson."

She served my coffee at a window table, but I told her I'd hold off on the pie until Jack arrived. The woman glanced at the electric clock on the wall. It was quarter-to-ten, about the time Jack usually came in for his daily fix. Fifteen minutes later she refilled my coffee mug and said, "I don't know where that boy could be." At ten fifteen she served me a slice of pie that made me question Jack's taste and a third cup of coffee. By ten thirty the woman was pacing. You might have thought she was Jack's worried mother. I was starting to become anxious myself.

At ten forty I said, "I bet Jack is at home waiting for me. Maybe he thought we'd meet there and then go out for pie."

The woman looked at me like I had just tracked mud into her kitchen.

"Don't you think you should find out?" she told me.

* * *

Snow continued to fall but it was nearly thirty-five degrees and the flakes melted on contact with my windshield while I drove west on Summit Avenue. I had my wipers going but they couldn't do anything about the hard gray sky or the dark, dreary woods. Jack and Tess had a place overlooking the Sand Hill River. To reach it I had to turn off the blacktop and follow a sand and gravel driveway that meandered nearly a quarter mile through the forest—Tess would rather go around a tree than cut it down. At the end of the driveway I found all the bright lights I could want: red, blue and white. They flickered silently from the bars on top of the Polk County Sheriff Department cruisers that blocked my way. I counted them: one, two, three. I had been a reporter long enough to know that three cop cars meant serious trouble.

I parked my car and dashed the rest of the way to the house, slipping and sliding in the melting snow, but not falling. The garage door was open and Jack's SUV and Tess' Audi were parked inside—Jack's golf clubs were leaning against the wall. I could have reached the back door through the garage, but went to the front instead. I pounded on the door. A deputy opened it like it was a great inconvenience to him.

"Who are you?" he wanted to know. His nametag read B. Hermundson.

"Danny?" Tess was sitting on a sofa beyond him next to a female deputy. "Danny," she called again.

I brushed past the deputy as Tess left the sofa and rushed straight into my arms. "Oh. Danny," she moaned, her face pressed hard against my chest. I embraced her even as a deputy with chevrons on his sleeve shook his head - a message to Deputy Hermundson at the door I guessed.

"Tess, what's happened?" I said. "Where's Jack?"

"I don't know. Last night... He... Danny, Jack has disappeared."

She felt my body tense, felt my arms release her shoulders. Her eyes found mine.

"Danny?"

"What do you mean, 'Jack has disappeared.'"

"He wasn't here when I came home last night. I haven't seen him since I went to work Monday morning."

I stepped away from her, moving backward until I bumped into the deputy.

"Tess, what did you do?"

"What do you mean?"

"Sir." The sergeant slid past Tess. "Sir, could you identify yourself."

"Daniel Thorn. I'm a reporter with the Minneapolis *Star Tribune.*"

"Why are you here, sir?"

"Jack Edelson is my friend. My best friend. He asked me to meet him at ten this morning at the Eats 'N' Antiques. I came here when he didn't show."

"Why did he want to meet you?"

"He was afraid."

"Afraid of what?"

58

"He said his wife was plotting to kill him."

"What?" Tess moved between the sergeant and myself. "What did you say?"

"Jack said you were plotting to kill him because you discovered he was having an affair. He said you took out a half million dollar life insurance policy on him."

I didn't think it was possible for a woman to hit a man as hard as Tess hit me. She caught me just to the left of the point of my chin and snapped my head back so violently I thought my neck was broken. I left my feet and flew against the door—I would have fallen if the Deputy Hermundson hadn't braced me by the shoulders.

The sergeant didn't seem to mind. He gently guided Tess by the elbow back to the sofa.

"Is it true, Mrs. Edelson, what your friend says?" the sergeant asked.

"He's not my friend. And of course it's not true. I would never hurt my husband. Never. You have to..."

The sergeant squatted next to Tess and patted her knee. "It's okay," he said. He glanced over his shoulder at me.

"I only know what Jack told me," I said.

"Mrs. Edelson, is your husband having an affair?" The sergeant asked the question with as much sympathy as he could muster, but it sounded like a slap in the face just the same.

"Absolutely not. How dare you?" Tess glared at me. "Jack loves me."

"Mrs. Edelson..."

"He does."

"Mrs. Edelson, I need you to do something for me. A favor. I need you to go upstairs and go through your husband's belongings. His razor. His toothbrush. Clothes he might wear. A suitcase he might pack. I need to know…"

"This is ridiculous."

"When you called, you said your husband might have been kidnapped. That's why we dispatched three units. I need to be sure that he didn't leave of his own free will before we investigate further."

Tess glared at me some more. She leaped so quickly to her feet that the sergeant fell backwards. "Fine," she said and rushed upstairs. The sergeant and I followed.

Tess went first to the bathroom where she opened and slammed a cabinet door and threw a toothbrush cup that shattered in her bathtub. She went to a bureau in her bedroom, opened one drawer, then the next, then the next; starting at the bottom and working upward like a burglar. Finally, she yanked open a closet door, rifled the jackets and slacks and dress shirts hanging inside and kicked something on the floor.

"It's true," she said. She closed the closet door and rested her forehead against it. "Oh, God, it's true. My husband left me."

Tess slowly sank into a puddle on the floor, her voice singing an aria of anguish and pain that the sergeant couldn't silence with all the "there, theres" in the world.

All in all, I thought it was a fine job of acting.

* * *

It took a while before Tess was calm enough to answer questions. She was again sitting on her sofa surrounded by the deputies. The female deputy— her nametag read C. Moore—kept repeating "It'll be all right," but I don't think she believed it.

"Who was Jack having an affair with?" I asked. I already knew the answer, but I wanted her to say it.

"Leave me alone, Danny, can't you?"

"No, I can't. Who was he having an affair with?"

"That's enough, buddy," said the sergeant.

"You're thinking Jack ran off with his girl," I told the sergeant. "You think this is just a domestic matter and the police shouldn't be involved. If that's true, then why is Jack's SUV parked inside the garage?"

From the expression on his face, the sergeant thought that was a good question.

"Mrs. Edelson, I need to know," he said. "Who was Mr. Edelson involved with?"

Tess stared at him for a long time while her face registered the five steps of the grieving process from denial to acceptance. Finally, she exhaled slowly and said, "Jodi Bakken."

Tess spoke the name so softly I could barely hear it. But the sergeant heard just fine. He stood straight and crossed his arms over his chest, a classic defensive posture.

"Who?" asked the sergeant.

"Jodi Bakken, all right?" Tess answered, choking out the words. I had the distinct impression that she would have been a lot happier if Jack had been kidnapped.

"Are you sure?" he wanted to know.

Tess nodded.

"Do you know her?" I asked the sergeant.

"She's married to one of our deputies."

I followed the sergeant outside; told him I wanted to be there when he interviewed Jodi Bakken. He didn't like the idea and I had to give him the old indignant reporter routine—"what do you have to hide?" A Twin Cities cop probably would have blown me off. But the sergeant didn't have much experience with the press and I convinced him that terrible things would happen if he left me out of the loop. Finally, he agreed, only he told me I had to take my own car. "I ain't running no taxi service for muckrakers," he said. Before we left I made him tell me about Deputy Bakken.

"Professionally, he's very good at his job," the sergeant said. "He's one of the few deputies we have who's willing to do knock and talks."

"Knock and talks?"

"About seventy-five percent of Minnesota's meth labs are outstate. People cook their crank out here because it's easier to get farm fertilizer and other ingredients, because distant neighbors are less likely to smell the odor and because there are plenty of places to dump the waste—a pound of crank yields about seven-eight pounds of hazardous waste. The problem is so big and there are so few of us—a dozen patrol officers and one investigator—that whenever we hear about a lab, we'll do a knock and talk. We'll show up at the suspect's door and warn them to shut down, leave or prepare to be arrested. And it usually works. These people are so paranoid it's easy to drive them out."

"Deputy Bakken is good at these knocks and talks?" I asked.

"He's fearless. See, these people, these meth users, they're unpredictable and completely dangerous. Yeah, you can drive a lot of them out with a stern lecture. But the rest—their aggression is far above and beyond any other drug users. There are more guns, more explosives, more violence. Most of us don't want to deal with them. But Deputy Bakken, he just goes up there and does his thing. Mostly he goes alone."

"Alone?"

"I know what you're thinking. Maybe Bakken says and does things that maybe he shouldn't. But because of him we have control of our meth problem. There are still dealers our here, still labs, I'm sure of it. But you don't see it like you do in other counties."

"You said professionally Bakken's good at his job," I reminded the sergeant. "What about personally?"

"Off the record?"

"Sure."

"Personally, he's an asshole."

* * *

Deputy Bakken lived in a double-wide trailer in a large clearing deep in the woods on the other side of two railroad tracks. It was a nice looking trailer, well kept up, with a wooden deck leading to the front door. But there was an unsightly pit of dirt and ash and melted snow about a dozen steps in front of the wooden steps where someone, probably Bakken, recently had a large fire. The sergeant parked in the driveway and I parked directly behind him. An old, single-car garage stood at the top of the driveway with a window in the door. In front of the garage was another Polk County Sheriff Department cruiser. The country supplied a cruiser to its deputies and encouraged them to use it. "Everyone's on call twenty-four-seven," the sergeant said.

I went to the garage and peeked through the window. Inside was an old Buick Regal. I told the sergeant and he said, "Jodi's." We followed the shoveled path from the driveway to the wooden deck. Deputy Bakken answered our knock almost immediately.

"Sarge, what are you doing here?" Bakken asked. He gave me a hard look, but didn't ask for an introduction.

"Truth is, Deputy, we came to speak with Jodi. Is she in?"

The sergeant moved to step through the doorway, but Bakken blocked his path.

"Jodi? What do you need to talk to her for? Have people been sayin' somethin'? Has she been sayin' somethin'? I got a right to know."

Bakken spoke quickly and used his hands to punctuate every other word. I thought he was acting as paranoid as the crank heads he dealt with. The sergeant didn't seem to notice.

"It's about Jack Edelson," the sergeant said.

"The stock guy? What about him?"

"You know him?" I asked.

"I've seen him around."

"He's gone missing," the sergeant said.

"What's that got to do with Jodi?"

"We're hoping Jodi might be able to help us."

"Why would Jodi be able to help you with that? What's going on here? What's this about?"

"Where is your wife, Deputy Bakken?" I asked.

"Who are you?"

"Is she here?"

"No, she's not here."

"Where is Jodi?" the sergeant asked.

"Visiting her sister Joanne in Fargo."

"Joanne what?" I asked.

"Joanne Farmer. Who are you?"

"Is that her car in the garage?" I asked.

"What of it?"

"When did Jodi leave?" the sergeant asked.

"Yesterday morning."

The sergeant set his hand on Bakken's shoulder. "We need to talk," he said. The deputy brushed the hand away.

"Talk about what?"

The sergeant gestured at me to get lost. I told him, "I'll meet you at Eats 'N' Antiques." As he nudged his deputy back inside the trailer, I moved off the deck and casually walked over packed snow to the fire pit. A chunk of pale plastic caught my eye and I retrieved it from the ashes. It was the body of a Barbie doll, the head torn off. I tossed it back into the pit, moved to Bakken's cruiser and leaned against it while I studied the trailer. After a few moments to build up my courage, I slipped around to the driver's side, opened the door, and used the lever below the seat to pop the trunk. A few minutes later I was backing my own car out of the driveway.

I drove about a hundred fifty yards to a crossroads, hung a left and parked, hoping the sergeant wouldn't notice the car when he left. I abandoned the vehicle and made my way on foot through the woods back to the edge of the clearing overlooking Bakken's trailer. I was just in time. Before I had a chance to settle in, Bakken and the sergeant emerged from the trailer, stood and chatted for a few minutes on the wooden deck. They shook hands and the sergeant went to his cruiser. Bakken watched him drive off from the deck.

I gave it a slow count after the sergeant was out of sight. At twenty-seven seconds, Bakken leapt from the deck and dashed into his garage. He came out a moment later carrying a small spade, ran behind the trailer and disappeared into the woods, moving fast. I noted the time on my watch. Less than fifteen minutes later he returned, walking casually and smiling, the spade slung over his shoulder. He returned the shovel to the garage before disappearing back into the trailer. I circled to my right, keeping out of sight, until I cut his trail. A double set of footprints in the fresh snow—they weren't difficult to follow.

It was an hour before I was able to join the sergeant at Eats 'N' Antiques. He was walking out as I was walking in.

"I waited for you," he told me, his mood foul.

"I'm sorry," I said. "There was something I had to do."

"Bakken is all broke up about his wife. I hope you're satisfied."

"Not really, but then it takes a lot to satisfy me."

"Jodi Bakken and Jack Edelson running off together isn't a criminal matter," the sergeant said. "I don't see how it makes much of a newspaper story, either."

"If that's what happened."

"You know something I don't?"

"Did you talk to the sister, Joanne Farmer?"

"No. Why should I?"

"Because she has an interesting story to tell."

I retrieved my cell phone from my pocket, hit the re-dial button. A moment later, Joanne Farmer answered. I had spoken to her during my drive from Bakken's place to Eats 'N' Antiques.

"Ms. Farmer, this is Daniel Thorn. Could you please tell the sergeant everything you told me?" I handed the sergeant the cell. He asked the woman the same questions I had and while I couldn't hear her voice, I knew what her answers would be.

She told the sergeant that Jodi had not come to visit her, that a visit had not been planned and that she was worried about her.

"When was the last time you spoke to Jodi?" the sergeant asked.

"Three days ago, the last time that creep beat on her."

"Bakken beat her?"

"He's been abusing her for years. Last time he burnt her collection of Barbie's."

"What happened?"

"Who knows? Maybe he didn't like the way Jodi grilled his steak. Maybe his beer wasn't cold enough. Maybe he has serious self-esteem issues and whenever he doesn't get the respect he thinks he deserves from the people he works with, from the people on the street, he takes it out on Jodi. Only this time he not only beat her, he destroyed her collection of Barbie dolls - Jodi's been collecting Barbies since she was a little girl. She loved those dolls. Sergeant, my sister is a beautiful woman both inside and out. She deserves a lot better than getting beat on by that, that creep."

"I understand."

"Do you? Than you can do me a favor. If my sister ran off with some guy who treats her decent, don't find her."

After he finished his conversation, the sergeant returned the cell and I deactivated it.

"Come with me," he said.

* * *

The sergeant drove us to Bridges Medical in Ada. The admitting nurse confirmed what Joanne Farmer had told us—Bakken regularly abused his wife. Jodi had been treated for major contusions, sprains and a few fractures over a three-year period.

"Why didn't you call the police?" the sergeant asked.

"Deputy Bakken is the police," the nurse replied. "And besides, as hard as we tried to make her say it, Mrs. Bakken refused to admit she had been abused. She insisted her injuries were the result of an accident. Forty percent of the women we treat in emergency rooms are sent there by husbands and boyfriends and it's always an accident."

"That's probably why Bakken acted all paranoid before," the sergeant said when we were back in the cruiser. "He thought someone, maybe Jodi, had dimed him out."

"Unless he has some other reason to be upset by a visit from the cops," I told him.

"What are you getting at?"

"You know what I'm getting at."

"First Mrs. Edelson killed her husband, now Deputy Bakken killed his wife."

"Yes."

"Like most reporters I've met, you have a vivid imagination."

"Think so?"

We were in Highway 32, following the railroad tracks as we drove south to Fertile. Without warning, the sergeant pulled off the highway onto the shoulder and halted. He rolled down his window. The snow had stopped and the sky was clearing. Cool, crisp air filled the car.

"What do we know?" he asked.

"You tell me," I said.

"It looks to me like two lovers ran off together, deserting their spouses. The only reason I'm sitting here now is because there's the suggestion that Mrs. Edelson was plotting to kill her husband and Jodi's husband has a history of abusing her—which are two darn good motives for taking off, don't you think?"

"Bakken lied when he said Jodi went to visit her sister in Fargo."

"Not necessarily. That could've been what Jodi told him before she left and he believed it."

"Except her car is still in the garage. So is Jack's."

"Meaning what?"

"How did Jodi and Jack leave Fertile? Do you have airline service here? Buses? Amtrak?"

The sergeant shook his head. In the distance we could hear the mournful whine of a railroad whistle.

"Do you think they hopped a freight?" I asked.

"Maybe they had help."

"Maybe they never left."

"We need a little more evidence before we start saying that."

"If this was the Twin Cities, the cops would be all over it - the beautiful wife of an abusive police officer disappears, are you kidding? Forget the local media. CNN, Fox News, every tabloid in the country would be in your face demanding to know what the hell you're doing about it."

"This isn't the Twin Cities," the sergeant said.

"What's it going to take for you to bring Bakken in for questioning? To get a warrant to search his place? A dead body on the street corner?"

Apparently, that was exactly what it was going to take. The sergeant made noises about issuing a missing persons bulletin, monitoring credit card usage, contacting the Social Security Administration, even placing a notice in the American Hotel Association monthly newsletter, but what it amounted to was this: the Polk County Sheriff's Department did not have jurisdiction to look for two lovers on the lam from their spouses. Unless it uncovered physical evidence that a crime was committed, it was inclined to look the other way.

Like many a poor gambler, I had overplayed my hand.

But then I got lucky.

The Winnebago blew up.

From what we were able to piece together later, every month a Hispanic and his Dakota partner would drive from Mason City in Iowa, to La Crosse and Eau Claire in Wisconsin, up to Duluth in Minnesota, across to Grand Forks and Fargo in North Dakota, down to Sioux Falls and Sioux City in South Dakota, then back to Mason City, scrupulously avoiding major metropolitan areas and their police departments. They'd stop for only a few days in each city, crank up a clan lab in the back of their fully-loaded RV, cook a few pounds of meth, sell limited quantities to a select circle of low-profile dealers, then hit the road again. Since they were on wheels, they'd be in and out of a police jurisdiction before the local heat even knew they were there. Sweet. Except this time the boys were careless storing their chemicals in the back of the Winnebago. While cutting through Polk County on their way to Grand Forks, they encountered a pothole and the meth lab exploded.

We found them a few clicks east of Highway 32 on CR 12, what remained of their RV was laying on its side across the blacktop. The two deputies I had met earlier—Hermundson and Moore—were already on the scene by the time we arrived. So were the Fertile volunteer fire brigade and Polk County EMS.

The Dakota was toast; the EMTs had already draped a blanket over his body. The Hispanic was badly burned on his arms, torso and face. He was crying as they loaded him into the blue and white van, but not for mercy, medical attention, or even his lawyer. He wanted to see Deputy Bakken.

"'E's my friend."

"Your friend?" said the sergeant.

Maybe the Hispanic was delirious with pain and that is why he was making what the courts call "spontaneous declarations." Most likely he saw the police uniforms and figured they were all his friends.

"'E show me good place ta camp," the Hispanic said. "Good place ta cook my goods. Dep'ty Bakken my friend."

From the expression on his face, I had the distinct impression the sergeant no longer felt that way about Bakken, if he ever had.

"I want him here, now," he snapped at the female deputy.

They paged him, radioed and called on a land line. Only Deputy Bakken wasn't answering.

I looked upward. The clouds had parted and the sky had become a pale blue. It was turning into a beautiful day.

Three Polk County Sheriff department cruisers rushed into the clearing surrounding Bakken's trailer only to find a fourth cruiser in the driveway. Unfortunately, Bakken was long gone, and so was the Buick Regal that had been parked in the garage. The sergeant ordered an alert for the Regal. Afterward, he told Moore to search the cruiser while he and Hermundson checked out the trailer. I remained with Moore. I had managed to tag-along with the deputies mostly by pretending I wasn't there and I stayed way back while she meticulously examined the contents of the cruiser. I didn't speak a word until she popped the trunk.

"What's that?" I said.

"What's what?"

"That smell."

Deputy Moore sniffed the air.

"It smells like—that's perfume." Moore leaned into the trunk. "Oh, no," she said, followed by, "Sergeant."

She explained quickly when he returned to the driveway.

"The trunk smells of a woman's fragrance—I think it's called Obsession." As if on cue, Deputy Hermundson returned to the trailer.

"Something else," Moore said. "Along the inside of the trunk lid—I think that's blood and human hair."

The sergeant reached over and slammed the trunk closed.

"Don't touch anything else," he said. "Have the car towed to our impound lot, then call the Bureau of Criminal Apprehension and ask them to send a forensics team up here."

"Yes, sir," said Moore.

"Sergeant," said Hermundson. The deputy had returned from the trailer. He was holding a small bottle of Obsession in his hand.

The sergeant looked like he was about to be sick. His expression became even worse when his radio crackled. The Buick Regal had been spotted moving at high speed on Summit Avenue toward Sand Hill River.

"Tess," I said aloud.

I had been surprised by how calmly and efficiently the deputies moved up on the scene—I had expected Barney Fife but got Steve McGarrett, instead.

It was only about five thirty, but night was already a reality. Yet in winter it's never entirely dark. The snow and ice always find one source or another of illumination to magnify and reflect and the night sky was loaded with them—stars you rarely see in the light-polluted Twin Cities. They made the area around the Edelson house seem as bright to me as Midway Stadium during a night game and I felt terribly exposed as we moved to the front.

Light also poured from the house; it fell like a blanket on the snow that laid beyond the large bay window overlooking the river. Inside, we could plainly see Tess tied to the arms of a chair. Her face was so mottled with fear and exhaustion that I scarcely recognized her. Bakken paced in front of her, talking loudly and waving his hands.

The sergeant sent Hermundson to the far side of the house and positioned Moore closer to the bay window. Both deputies were carrying .308 hunting rifles fitted with telescopes.

Moore sighted on Bakken.

"I can take him now," she said.

The sergeant rested a hand on her shoulder.

"Don't fire unless you need to," he said. The sergeant removed his gun belt and set it next to Moore's knee. "I'm going to try and negotiate with him."

Bakken turned his back to Tess and walked to the window. I thought for sure that he had seen us until he brought his hand up to shield his eyes from the light and I realized that we could easily see in, but because of the reflections, he couldn't see out.

I sighed deeply and both the sergeant and Deputy Moore looked at me like they were surprised I was there.

"Be quiet," the sergeant said. "Stay the hell out of the way."

I nodded my agreement, afraid to speak.

"Jeezus," he muttered and started making his way toward the front door. He couldn't have taken more than a half dozen steps when we all heard Bakken scream, "I want my money!" loud enough to penetrate the walls of the house and echo across the snow.

The sergeant looked up; saw Bakken take his county-issued Glock from his pocket and point it with both hands at Tess.

"I want my money now!"

"Deputy," the sergeant said.

It was early morning before they finally removed Bakken's body from the house, before the ME, the county attorney, the county sheriff and a field agent for the Bureau of Criminal Apprehension ran out of questions to ask. One question in particular still hung in the air: What did Bakken mean when he said, "I want my money."

With a loud, sustained sob, Tess collapsed into the sergeant's arms—it was like the question had given her permission to cry. The sergeant seemed embarrassed as he gently maneuvered her to the sofa. He wrapped her arms around Tess and held her close. Tess rested her head against his shoulder and wept. After a few minutes she began talking. She said, "He told me he killed Jack. He said he found Jack and Jodi together and he killed them both. He said he did it as a favor to me, but now the police were after him. He said he heard it on his police radio. He said he needed money and he wanted me to give him some. He wanted me to pay him for killing my husband." She cried throughout most of her answer and when she finished, all restraint left her. She wept until the sergeant's shirt was wet with her tears.

And I thought, Tess was more than a good actor. She was way up there with Meryl Streep and Cate Blanchett.

"You don't believe this, do you?" I asked the sergeant. "Tess and Bakken were in this together. Don't you get it? Bakken came here to get his money and Tess wouldn't give it to him."

"What money?" the sergeant asked.

"The percentage of the insurance settlement Tess promised to give him for killing her husband."

It was then that the sergeant decided he had had more than enough of me for one day and threw me out of the house.

To prove I was full of crap, Tess agreed to take a computerized polygraph exam conducted by John Hopkins University. According to the Applied Physics Laboratory Computer Scoring Algorithm— whatever the hell that was—the probability was greater than ninety-nine percent that the subject was being truthful when she answered "No" to the questions "Did you conspire with Deputy Bakken to kill your husband?" and "Are you responsible for the death of your husband?" Despite my protests, the BCA cleared her as a suspect.

DNA testing proved that the hair found in the trunk of Deputy Bakken's cruiser belonged to Jodi Bakken and the blood belonged to Jack Edelson. Based on that and Tess' testimony, the Office of the Polk County Coroner concluded that they were both dead and classified their deaths as homicides. Despite an extensive search, their bodies were never found.

A few weeks later Tess and I met in the office of a probate attorney in Crookston, Minnesota, the seat of power in Polk County. According to the will he read, Jack left his thirty-five hundred dollar golf clubs to me. He left everything else to Tess—an estate valued at over seven hundred grand including his half of their joint property. Tess and I thanked the lawyer. As we left his office, Tess said she had Jack's clubs in the trunk of her car. I transferred them to my car.

"What are you going to do?" I asked her.

"I already put in my notice at the hospital; my house will go on the market tomorrow. The realtor thinks I'd be better off waiting until the weather gets warmer but I don't want to wait. I want to sell the house, sell the furniture and get out of here just as soon as I can."

"What about Jack's life insurance?"

"The state declared Jack dead, a victim of homicide. My lawyer doesn't think there'll be a problem with the insurance company."

"Lucky you."

"Are you driving back to the Cities tonight?"

"I think that would be best."

"You could come down to Fertile; stay in the guest room like you did during the holidays."

"If I did that, people might think we actually like each other."

"We certainly can't have that, can we?"

"Besides, you've been a widow for less than a month. What would Jack say?"

"I think Jack is past caring, don't you?"

I carried Jack's golf bag through my back door into the kitchen. Jodi met me there with a spatula in her hand and wearing a white apron.

"Hi," she said cheerfully.

Jodi looked a little like the Barbie dolls she used to collect, except for the bruises on her face, neck and arms where Deputy Bakken had beaten her. But they had already faded to a soft yellow and would soon be gone forever.

Jack appeared in the doorway behind Jodi and went to the golf bag, taking it from my hands.

"How did it go?" he asked.

"According to plan."

"Is it in here?" Jack opened zippers and flaps. Instead of balls, tees, shoes, rain gear and other golfing paraphernalia, thousands of dollars spilled out, most of the money in packets held together by rubber bands.

"Wow," Jack said. "How much is here?"

"I didn't count it," I said. "I was in a hurry. Bakken kept the money in a lock box buried in the woods behind his trailer. The box was designed to keep the contents safe in case of fire or flood or whatever. It wasn't hard to open. I took the money from the box, ran it over to your place and stashed it in the golf bag before meeting the sergeant."

"How did you know where it was?" Jodi asked. "Even I didn't know where it was—he made sure of that."

"The first thing Bakken did when he realized that you left him was to check to see if you took his money. I knew he would. I was watching."

"Four hundred sixty-seven thousand dollars," Jack said after he finished counting. "That's more than I had hoped for."

"If the Polk County Sheriff's Department ever starts arresting some of those meth dealers instead of just chasing them down the road to another jurisdiction, they'll probably find that Bakken had been taking money from them for years."

"I want you to take some of this—you did all the work."

I shook my head. "I didn't do it for the money."

"You did it for us," said Jodi.

"What can I say? I'm a sucker for love."

"I kinda feel sorry for Tess, though," Jodi said.

"Don't be," said Jack. "She has all that insurance money to keep her warm."

"But she doesn't have you."

Jack and Jodi embraced. I poured myself a cup of coffee.

"You will look in on Tess, won't you, Danny?" Jack asked. "Once in a while just to make sure she's all right."

"Sure."

"You're a good friend. I think I'm going to miss you most of all."

Jack hugged me.

"Do you want to know the names we've chosen?" Jodi asked.

"No," I said. I hugged her - there was a lot of hugging going on in my kitchen. "Just have a good life, both of you."

An hour later they were gone, driving south in an aging Ford Escort I had bought at a charity auction and registered under a false name. It was the same car I had planted in the parking lot of the Fertile-Beltrami High School for Jack and Jodi to escape in. A few minutes later, I called Fertile, Minnesota.

"Hi," I said when Tess answered.

"Are they gone?" she asked.

"Just left."

"Will they be all right?"

"Bakken left them nearly a half million dollars. If they can't start over on that…"

"I kinda feel sorry for them."

"Don't be. They have each other to keep themselves warm."

"That leaves just you and me."

"I'll have plenty of closet space cleared out by the time you move in."

Author's Note: This is my favorite short story, a piece I wrote for the anthology Twin Cities Noir. *The editors, Julie Schaper and Steven Horwitz, told me they made it the lead story because "it was the most noirish." I really like that.* The Twin Cities Daily Planet *wrote: "Minnesota Book Award winner, David Housewright's 'Mai-Nu's Window' opens the collection. A shy Puerto Rican teenage boy and a Hmong woman going to law school are Frogtown neighbors. The unexpected consequences of their encounter reveals the challenges of immigrant tradition and American assimilation, with subtle perfection, echoing classic themes from James M. Cain". I really like that, too.*

Mai-Nu's Window

Benito Hernandez did not know when Mai-Nu began leaving her window shade up. Probably when the late August heat had first arrived—dog days in Minnesota. It was past ten thirty PM yet the temperature was eighty-six degrees Fahrenheit in Benito's bedroom and his windows, too, were wide open and his shades up. Just as they were in most of the houses in his neighborhood. That was one way to tell the rich from the poor in the Land of 10,000 Lakes. The ones who could afford central air, all their windows were closed.

The window faced Benito's room. Through it he could see most of Mai-Nu's living room as well as a sliver of her bedroom. Mai-Nu was in her living room now, sitting on a rust-colored sofa, her bare feet resting on an imitation wood coffee table. She was stripped down to a white, sleeveless scoop-neck tee and panties. What little fresh air that seeped through the window screen was pushed around by an electric fan that swung slowly in a half circle and droned monotonously. It didn't offer much relief. Benito could see strands of raven-black hair plastered to Mai-Nu's forehead and a trickle of sweat running down between her breasts. Next to her on the sofa were a bowl of melting ice, a half-gallon carton of orange juice and a liter of Phillips vodka. She was reading a book while she drank. Occasionally, she would mark passages in the book with a yellow highlighter.

Less than five yards separated their houses and sometimes Benito could hear Mai-Nu's voice; could hear the music she played and the TV programs she watched. Sometimes he felt he could almost reach out and touch her. It was something he wanted very much to do. Touch her. But she was twenty-three, a student at William Mitchell Law School—it was a law book that she was reading. Benito was sixteen and about to begin his junior year in high school. She was Hmong. He was Hispanic.

Still, Benito was convinced Mai-Nu was the most beautiful woman he had ever known. A long feminine neck, softly molded moon face, alluring oval eyes, pale flesh that glistened with perspiration—she was forever wrestling with her long, thick hair and often she would tie it back in a ponytail as she had that night. Watching her made him feel tumescent, made his body tingle with sexual electricity, even though the few times he had actually seen her naked were so fleeting as to be more illusion than fact. Often he would imagine the two of them together. And just as often he would berate himself for this. It was wrong, it was stupid, it was *asqueroso!* Yet when night fell, he would hide himself in the corner of his bedroom and watch, the door locked, the lights off, telling his parents that he was doing homework or listening to music.

Mai-Nu mixed a drink, her second by Benito's count, and padded in the direction of her tiny kitchen. She was out of sight for a few moments, causing Benito alarm, as it always did when she slipped from view. When Mai-Nu returned, she was carrying a plate of leftover pork stew with corn bread topping. The meal had been a gift from Juanita Hernandez. Benito's mother was always doing that, making far too much food then parceling it out to her neighbors. She had brought over a platter of *carne y pollo* when Mai-Nu first arrived as a house-warming gift. Benito had accompanied her and was soon put to work helping Mai-Nu move in.

It wasn't much of a place, he had noted sadly. The living room was awash in forest green except for a broad water stain on the wall behind the couch that was gray. Burnt orange drapes framed the windows and the carpet was once blue but now resembled the water stain. The kitchen wasn't much better. The walls were painted a sickly pink and the linoleum had the deep yellow hue of urine. Just off the living room was a tiny bathroom: sink, toilet, tub—no shower—and beyond that a tiny bedroom.

There was no yard. The front door opened onto three concrete steps that ended at the sidewalk. The boulevard between the sidewalk and curb was hard-packed dirt and exactly as wide as eight of Benito's size ten-and-a-half sneakers. Mai-Nu had no garage either, only a strip of broken asphalt next to the house that was too small for her ancient Ford LTD.

"It is only temporary," Mai-Nu had told Juanita. "My parents came from Laos. My father had helped fight for the CIA during the war. They did well after they arrived in America—they owned two restaurants. But they believed in the traditions of their people, so when my parents were killed in a car accident, it was my father's older brother who inherited their wealth. He was supposed to raise my brother and I. Now that we are both of age, the property should come to us."

But six months had passed. The property had not come to them and Mai-Nu was still there.

Benito wondered about that while he watched her eat. Mai-Nu did not have a job as far as he knew, unless you would call attending law school a job. Possibly her uncle helped her pay the rent on her house, such as it was. Or maybe it was her brother—Cheng Song was not much older than Benito, but he had quit school long ago and was now the titular head of the Hmongolian Boy's Club, a street-gang with a reputation for terror. They had met only once. Outside of Mai-Nu's. She had been shouting at him, telling a smirking Cheng that he was wasting his life when Benito had arrived home carrying his hockey equipment. He was only a sophomore, yet his booming slapshot had already caught the notice of both pro and college scouts alike. Several D-1 schools had indicated that they might offer him a scholarship if he improved his defense and kept his grades up, which Juanita vowed he would do—*"Si no saca buena noto le mato!"* Cheng hadn't seemed impressed by the hockey player, but later he told Benito, "You watch out for my sister. Anything happen, you tell me."

Mai-Nu took the remains of her dinner back to the kitchen. When she returned she mixed a third drink and retrieved her law book. She kept glancing at her watch as if she were expecting a visitor. The phone rang, startling both her and Benito. Mai-Nu went to answer it, slipping out of sight.

There was a mumbling of hellos and then something else. "Yes, Pa Chou," Mai-Nu said, her voice rising in volume. And then, "No, Uncle." She was shouting now. "I will not."

Benito wished he could see her. He moved around his bedroom, hoping to get a better sight angle into Mai-Nu's house, but failed.

"I know, I know...But I am not Hmong, Pa Chou. I am American...But I am, Uncle. I am an American woman...I will not do what you ask. I will not marry this man...In Laos you are clan leader. In America you are not."

She slammed the receiver so hard against the cradle that Benito was sure she had destroyed her phone. A moment later Mai-Nu reappeared, her face flushed with anger. She guzzled her vodka and orange juice, made another drink and guzzled that.

Benito wished she would not drink so much.

* * *

The next morning, Benito found Mai-Nu at the foot of her front steps, stretching her long legs. She was wearing blue jogging shorts and a tight, white half-tee that emphasized her chest - at least that is what he noticed first. He was startled when she spoke to him.

"Benito," she said. *"Nyob zoo sawv ntyov."*

"Huh?"

"It means 'good morning.'"

"Oh. *¡Buenos dias!*"

"I'm probably going to melt in this heat, but I really need to exercise."

"It is hot."

"Well, I will see you..."

"Mai-Nu?"

"Yes?"

Benito was curious about the phone call the evening before, but knew he couldn't ask about it. Instead, he said, "Your name. What does it mean?"

"My name? It means 'gentle sun.'"

"That's beautiful."

Mai-Nu smiled at the compliment. Suddenly, she seemed interested in him.

"And Cheng Song?" Benito asked.

"Cheng, his first name, that means 'important' and my brother certainly wishes he were. Song is our clan name. The Hmong did not have last names until the West insisted on it in 1950s and many of us took our clan names. I am Mai-Nu Song."

"What about Pa Chou?"

"Where did you hear my uncle's name?"

Benito shrugged. "You must have told me."

"Hmm," Mai-Nu hummed. "Chou means 'rice steamer.'"

"Oh, yeah?"

She nodded. "'Pa' is a salutation of respect, like calling someone 'mister' or 'sir.'"

"Why does he have a salutation of respect?"

"Pa Chou is the leader of the Song clan in St. Paul. What that means—clan leaders are called upon to give advice and settle arguments within the clan."

"Like a *patron*. A godfather."

"Yes. Also," Mai-Nu's eyes grew dark and her voice became still, "also they arrange marriages and decide how much a groom's family must pay his bride's family to have her. Usually it is between six thousand and ten thousand dollars."

"Arranged marriages? Do you still do that?"

"The older community, my parent's generation, they really value the old Hmong culture. That is why they settled here in St. Paul. St. Paul has the largest urban Hmong population in the world. Close to twenty-five thousand of us. They come here because they can still be Hmong here. Do you understand?"

"I think so."

Benito attended a high school where thirty percent of the student body was considered minorities—African-Americans, Native-Americans, Asians, Somali, Indians, Latinos—all of them striving to maintain their identity in a community that was dominated by the Northern Europeans that first settled there.

"It is changing," said Mai-Nu. "The second generation, my generation, we are becoming American. But it is hard. Hard for the old ones to give up their traditions. Hard for the young ones, too, caught between cultures. My brother—he liked to have his freedom. I asked him, my uncle asked him, where do you go? What do you do? He says he is American so he can do whatever he likes. You cannot tell him anything. Now he is a gangster. He brings disgrace to the clan. Maybe if my parents were still alive…"

Mai-Nu shook her head, her ponytail shifting from one shoulder to the other.

Benito said, "What about you?"

"Me? I am bringing disgrace to the clan, too."

"I don't believe that."

"In my culture, a woman can only lead from behind. To be out front, to have a high profile, to be a lawyer—the old people, the clan leaders do not tolerate it. My uncle is very upset. He is afraid of losing power as the young people become more Americanized. Keeping me in my place, it is important to him. It proves that he is still in charge. That is why he wants me to marry."

"He arranged your marriage?"

"He is attempting to. He says—Pa Chou and my brother hate each other—but Pa Chou says he will leave all his wealth—my parents' wealth—to Cheng unless I agree to marry." She grinned then, an odd thing Benito thought. "My bride price—the last bid was twenty-two thousand. If they wait until after I get my law degree, the bidding will top twenty-five thousand."

"You are worth much more than that," Benito blurted.

Mai-Nu smiled at him. "You are very sweet," she said. And then, "I have to run if I am going to have time to get cleaned up before class."

A moment later she was moving at a steady pace down the street. Benito watched her.

"Gentle Sun," he said.

It was nearly ten PM when Mai-Nu went from her bedroom to her tiny bathroom—Benito saw her only for a moment. She was naked, but the rose-colored nightshirt she carried in front of her hid most of her body.

"¡Maldito sea!," Benito cursed.

Mai-Nu did not have a shower, Benito knew. Only a big, old-fashioned bathtub with iron feet. He imagined her soaking in the tub, white soap bubbles hugging her shoulders. But the image lasted only until he wiped sweat from his own forehead. It was so warm, he could not believe anyone would immerse themselves in hot water. So he flipped a channel in his head, and suddenly there was a picture of Mai-Nu standing in two inches of lukewarm water, giving herself a sponge bath. He examined the image closely behind closed eyes. Until he heard the sound of a vehicle coming quickly to a stop on the street.

His eyes opened in time to see three Asian men invade Mai-Nu's home. Flinging open the door and charging in, looking around like they were seeing the house for the first time. They were older than

Benito but smaller, the biggest about five-five, one hundred forty pounds.

One of the men called Mai-Nu's name.

"What do you want?" Mai-Nu shouted in reply.

She emerged from her bathroom. Her hair was dripping. The short-sleeve nightshirt she had pulled on was wet and clung to her body.

"I have come for you," the man replied.

"Get out."

"We will be married."

"I said no. Now get out."

"Mai-Nu…"

"Get out, get out."

The man reached for her and she punched him hard enough to snap his head back.

"You," the man said and grabbed for her. Mai-Nu darted away, but the other two men were there. They trapped her between them and closed on her, wrestled her writhing body into submission. Mai-Nu shouted a steady stream of what Benito guessed were Hmong curses while the first man begged her to remain still.

"It is for both our happiness," he said as they carried Mai-Nu toward the door.

Benito was running now, out of his bedroom, out of his house and toward Mai-Nu's front steps. He hit the first man out the door, leaping high with all his weight and momentum, catching the man with an elbow just under the chin, smashing him against the door frame, as clean a check as he had every thrown—his coach would have been proud.

The man bounced off the frame and crumbled to the sidewalk. The second man dropped Mai-Nu's legs and swung at Benito, but he danced away easily. He was more than a half dozen years younger than the three men, but five inches taller and thirty pounds heavier. And years of summer league had taught him how to throw a punch. But there were three of them.

"I called the cops," Benito shouted. "The cops are on their way."

Mai-Nu squirmed out of the third man's grasp and struck him hard in the face.

The man seemed mystified.

"But I love you," he said.

Mai-Nu hit him again.

The first two men turned toward Benito.

"The cops are coming," he repeated.

One of them said something that Benito could not understand. The other said, "We must leave," in clear English.

"Not without Mai-Nu," the third man said.

Mai-Nu shoved him hard and he nearly fell off the steps. His companions grabbed his shoulders and spoke rapidly to him as they dragged him to the van parked directly in front of Mai-Nu's house.

"Mai-Nu, Mai-Nu," he chanted as they stuffed him inside. A moment later they were driving off.

Mai-Nu watched them go, her hands clenched so tightly that her fingernails dug ugly half-moons into her palms.

Benito rested a hand on her shoulder.

"Are you okay?"

Mai-Nu spun violently toward him.

"Yes, I am okay."

Benito was startled by her anger and took a step backward. Mai-Nu saw the hurt expression in his face and reached for him.

"Benito, Benito," she chanted. "You were so brave."

She wrapped her arms around him and pulled him close. He could feel her exquisite skin beneath the wet nightshirt, could feel her breasts flatten against his chest.

"You are my very good friend," Mai-Nu said as she kissed his ear and his cheek. "My very good friend."

She released him and smiled so brightly, Benito put his hand on his heart, afraid that it had stopped beating.

"Are you all right?" Mai-Nu asked him.

Benito nodded his head.

"You are sure?"

Benito nodded again. After a moment, he found enough breath to ask, "Who were those men?"

"They are from the Kue clan."

"You know them?"

"Yes."

"What were they doing here? Why did they try to kidnap you?"

"It is called 'marriage by capture.'"

"What?"

"It is a Hmong custom. If a woman spends three days in a man's home, even if there is no physical contact between them, she must marry him as long as he can pay the bride price set by her family."

"By your uncle."

"It is becoming rare in America, but my uncle is desperate."

"That's crazy. I mean, they gotta know that you would turn them in, right? They have to know you'd have them arrested."

Mai-Nu did not answer.

"Right?"

"I could not do that to my people. For practicing a custom that has existed for hundreds of years, no I could not do that."

"But you wouldn't marry him?"

"You are very kind, Benito. And very brave. I am in your debt."

"Mai-Nu, you wouldn't marry him."

"I must ask you one more favor."

"Anything."

"You must not tell my brother about tonight. You must not tell him about my uncle. I know that he asked you to watch out for me, but you must not tell him anything. The way Cheng is, what he thinks of the old ways, you must not tell him. It would be very bad."

"Mai-Nu?"

"You must promise."

"I promise."

She embraced him; her lips found the side of his mouth. She said goodnight and returned to her house, locking the door behind her. Benito stood on the sidewalk for a long time, his fingers gently caressing the spot where Mai-Nu had kissed him.

* * *

It was a soft, cool night full of wishing stars, unusual for August in Minnesota—a summer evening filled with the promise of autumn—and Benito was terrified that the weather might encourage Mai-Nu to close her windows and lower her shade. As it was, she was dressed in blue Capri pants and a boxy white sweatshirt that revealed nothing of the body beneath. She was sitting on her front stoop, her back against the door, sipping vodka and orange juice.

Benito called to her from the sidewalk.

"Qué pa, ¡chica!" he said. *"¿Co'mo te va?"*

"Very well, thank you," Mai-Nu replied and patted the space next to her. Benito sat down.

"My Spanish is improving," she said.

"Si."

"I heard from a college, today," Benito said just to be saying something. "Minnesota State wants me to come down to Mankato and look at their campus."

Mai-Nu hugged Benito's arm and a jolt of electricity surged through his body.

"You will go far, I know you will," she told him.

"I need to get my scores up. I took a practice ACT test and only got a nineteen. Nineteen is borderline."

"It is hard, I know."

"Did you take the ACT?"

"Yes."

"How'd you do?"

"Thirty-one."

Benito's eyes widened in respect. Thirty-one put Mai-Nu in the top five percent in the country.

"I have always done well with tests," she told him.

Benito didn't know what to say to that so he said nothing. They sat together in silence, Mai-Nu still holding Benito's arm. She released it only when a Honda Accord slowed to a stop directly in front of them. Its lights flicked off, the engine was silenced. The man who stepped out of the vehicle was the largest Asian Benito had ever seen, nearly six feet tall. His jaw was square, his eyes unblinking—a military man, Benito decided. He smiled at Mai-Nu with a stern kindliness.

"You do not have a cordial word for your uncle?" he said.

"Why are you here?" Mai-Nu asked.

"We have much to talk about."

Benito started to rise. Mai-Nu reached for him, but Benito pulled his arm away.

"It is a private matter," he said and moved to his own stoop. It was only a dozen steps away; he didn't figure to miss much.

"Did you send those assholes last night?" Mai-Nu asked.

"Mai-Nu, your language…"

"Screw my language," she said and took a long pull of her drink.

Pa Chou's eyes became narrow slits. His voice was suddenly cold and hard.

"The way you drink," he said. "The way you talk. What has become of you?"

"I am angry, Pa Chou. Do you blame me?"

Pa Chou glanced around the street. Seeing Benito pretending not to listen, he said, "Let us go inside."

"Fine," said Mai-Nu. She stood and went into her house. Pa Chou followed. Benito gave them a head start, then dashed into his own house. His mother asked him what he was doing and he said he was going to his room to listen to music. Once there he stared intently through Mai-Nu's window, but could see neither her nor her uncle. But he could hear them. They spoke their native language. Benito did not have to understand their words to know they were angry.

He sat and listened for what seemed like a long time. Then he heard a distinct sound of skin slapping skin violently, followed by Mai-Nu falling into her living room. Pa Chou was there in an instant. He heaved her up by her arms, shook her like a doll and slapped her again with the back of his hand. Mai-Nu shouted at him and Pa Chou hit her again. Mai-Nu fell out of sight and Pa Chou followed. There were more shouts and more slapping sounds. Finally, Pa Chou strode purposely across the living room to the front door. He shouted something at Mai-Nu over his shoulder and left the house. Mai-Nu walked slowly into her living room and collapsed to her knees, leaning against the sofa. She covered her face with her arms and wept.

Benito closed his eyes and braced myself with both hands against his bureau. Something in his stomach flipped and flopped and tried to escape through his throat, but he choked it down. A blinding rage burned at the edge of his eyelids until teardrops formed. He smashed his fist against the side of the bureau, then shook the pain out of his hand.

It was a family matter, he told himself. It had nothing to do with him.

But he could tell Cheng Song about it.

He could do that.

The headline of the *St. Paul Pioneer Press* four days later read:

Killing underscores problems in growing Hmong community

The story suggested that the murder of Pa Chou Song and the subsequent arrest of Cheng Song by St. Paul police officers the next day was an indication of how difficult it is for many in the Hmong community to assimilate to American culture. But that is not what distressed Benito. It was the photograph of Pa Chou that the paper printed—a decidedly small man in his late forties standing next to the doorway of a Hmong restaurant.

Benito was confused. He rushed to Mai-Nu's house and knocked on her door.

"Who is it?" she called.

"Benito Hernandez," he answered through the screen door.

"Come in. Sit down. I will be there in a minute."

Benito entered the house and found a seat on the rust-colored sofa. There was a law book on the coffee table. Benito glanced at the spine—

Minnesota Statutes 2004. He opened it to the page held by a bookmark. A passage had been highlighted in yellow.

> *524.2-803 Effect of homicide on instate succession, wills, joint assets, life insurance and beneficiary designations.*
>
> *(a) A surviving spouse, heir or devisee who feloniously and intentionally kills the decedent is not entitled to any benefits under the will... Property appointed by the will of the decedent to or for the benefit of the killer passes as if the killer had predeceased the decedent.*

Mai-Nu had written something in the margin next to the passage with a fluid hand, and Benito turned the book to read it.

> *As only other living relative, I will inherit everything.*

Benito closed the book and returned it to the table when Mai-Nu entered the room. He stood to greet her. She appeared more radiant than at any time since he had known her. Her smile seemed like a gift to the world.

Mai-Nu was tying a white silk scarf around her head. She said, "It is traditional to wear a white headband when one is in mourning."

"Mourning for your uncle," Benito said.

"And my brother."

Benito was standing in front of her now, clutching the newspaper.

"Thank you for thinking of me." Mai-Nu gestured at the paper. "But I have already read it."

Benito showed her the photograph.

"This is your uncle?" he said.

"Yes."

"Pa Chou Song?"

"Yes, of course."

"It is not the man who came here that day. The man who beat you."

"You saw him beat me?"

"I saw…"

"Did you, Benito?"

Benito glanced at the open window and back at Mai-Nu.

"I saw," he said.

"And you told my brother?"

"I know now that you wanted me to tell Cheng what I saw."

"Did I?"

Benito nodded.

"There is no evidence of that."

"Evidence?"

"Did I tell you to go to my brother?"

"No."

"Did I tell *not* to speak to my brother."

"Yes."

"That is the evidence that the court will hear, should you go to court."

"I don't understand."

Mai-Nu brushed past Benito and retrieved the law book from the coffee table. She hugged it to her breasts.

"In Laos, women are expected to submit," she said. "Submit to their husbands, submit to their fathers, submit to their uncles. Not here. Here we are equal. Here we are protected by the law. I love America."

"Who was the man who came here that night?"

"A friend, Benito. Like you."

She reached out and gently stroked Benito's cheek.

"You must go now," she said.

A few minutes later, Benito returned to his bedroom. Dark and menacing storm clouds were rolling in from the northwest, laying siege to the sun and casting the world half in shadow. Mai-Nu's lights were on and though it was early morning, he had a good view of her living room.

He did not see her at first, then Mai-Nu appeared. She moved to the window and looked directly at him. She smiled and blew him a kiss. And slowly lowered her shade.

Author's Note: The Minnesota Crime Wave was back at it with an anthology called Resort to Murder. *This time, the concept was that each of the stories had to take place at one of Minnesota's countless resorts. I picked one on the shores of Lake Vermillon in the northern part of the state. I later asked my accountant if I could deduct my gambling losses from my taxes as a legitimate business deduction—it was research, after all. He didn't think that was a good idea. Oh, well. Something you should know—to a writer everything is material. Every place we go, every person we meet, every conversation we have could end up in a book or story. For example—the first nine lines of dialogue in this story were taken verbatim from a conversation with a waitress—and my sister-in-law—on a veranda of a restaurant in Minneapolis. The rest of the story, though, is purely fiction.*

Miss Behavin'

The waitress said, "That's a pretty ring."

Kathryn held her hand up and examined the ring like she was seeing it for the first time. The diamond sparkled in the light.

"Thank you," she said.

"How long have you kids been married?"

The question startled her. She flashed a panicked gaze at her companion sitting across the table.

"Thirteen years," he said.

"Good for you." The waitress finished refilling their water glasses and left to serve other customers. Kathryn watched her drift across the restaurant. A strand of black hair fell against her cheek when her head swung back to the table and she smoothed it into place.

"She thought we were married," Kathryn said.

"We are married," her companion said.

"But not to each other."

"A minor technicality."

"Is that all it is?"

"Kathryn, it's all perfectly innocent. If anyone asks—"

"Like your wife, Dr. Markham?"

"Yes, like my wife," Markham said. "If anyone asks, I'll tell them I met an interesting, intelligent woman during a seminar at a pharmaceutical convention and we had lunch together in plain sight of everyone. So, what do you think about the new Beta-blockers, Doctor?"

"I'm surprised you even remember what the seminar was about considering the way you kept staring at my legs."

"They are magnificent."

Markham liked the way Kathryn's cheeks flamed at the compliment, liked the way she smiled coyly and looked away. Doctors were all the same, he believed. No matter how generous, considerate or kindly they might seem, they were still doctors, which meant they were smarter than everyone else and sooner or later they would need to prove it. Kathryn was trying to prove it now, trying to prove how sophisticated and worldly she was. Like during the seminar when she noticed Markham noticing her. She leaned across two seats and whispered, "May I help you?"

"Just looking," Markham said.

"See anything you like?"

"One or two things, but I prefer to conduct a full examination before I make a final diagnosis."

"Perhaps a joint consultation is called for."

It was Kathryn who suggested lunch. The drug companies sponsoring the four-day convention insisted that the physicians and other guests attend all the morning seminars, yet afternoons and evenings were free for fun and frolic. Only Kathryn was over her head. To her surprise Markham had taken her flirting seriously and pressed hard. She would now either have to run for cover or make good on her innuendoes. Markham was betting on the latter. He had been convinced from the moment Kathryn walked into the meeting room and searched carefully before selecting his row, that she could be had.

"We're so lucky with the weather," Kathryn told him. "I expected northern Minnesota to be much colder. How far are we from Canada?"

"About forty miles as the crow flies."

"Where I come from, most people think Minnesota is somewhere up around the Arctic Circle. But it's really quite lovely."

"Lovely," Markham repeated. He was looking directly in her eyes when he said the word so she wouldn't be mistaken about what he meant. She smiled and glanced away again. Works every time, he told himself.

"Tell me about your wife," Kathryn said.

This time it was Markham's turn to look away. He wasn't embarrassed or surprised; sooner or later the question always came up. He was merely buying time while he selected the desired response:

soft, hard or harder? Some women preferred to hear nasty tales about the wife. They wanted to make sure they weren't breaking up a happy home. Markham thought it made being the other woman easier for them to bear. *Hey, the bitch deserves it.* Yet, Kathryn seemed different. The way she averted her eyes when he complimented her, the way she suddenly seemed fearful that they would be seen together, what the waitress would think—Kathryn was concerned with consequences. *First do no harm.* Soft, he decided.

"Susan is very smart, very beautiful and I love her more than I have words to tell," Markham said.

"But."

"Hmm?"

"I heard a 'but' in that sentence."

"You're a doctor," Markham said. "You know how punishing the profession can be. The hours. The interrupted dinners. The ruined holidays. At first it seemed like Susan enjoyed being a doctor's wife, yet after a few years she decided she needed more. She wanted to have her own identity, her own career. I was all for it. I encouraged her to go back to school; encouraged her to get her Masters. Only now it seems what she really wanted all along was to stop being a doctor's wife."

"Is that why you're flirting with a woman you barely know?"

"Well, it helps that the woman is lovely and smart." He was taking a helluva chance, Markham knew. Still, they were staying at a resort casino after all: slot machines, blackjack tables, poker rooms, even bingo. "Why are you flirting with a man you barely know?" he asked.

"Because..." She shook her head like it was a subject too painful to discuss. "Because the man is handsome and smart. Let it go at that."

"I didn't come here looking for a fling."

"But you could be talked into it."

"You could talk me into it."

"I haven't done—I've never tried to do anything like this before."

"Anything like what?"

"Seduce a man I don't know."

He shoots, he scores, Markham's inner voice shouted. "Well, it worked," he said aloud.

"Has it?"

"I know I'm having a very difficult time keeping my hands off you."

Kathryn glanced discreetly about the restaurant, trying to examine every face while pretending not to. Finally, she asked, "What are your plans for the rest of the day?"

"I was scheduled to play golf, but I'd rather spend time with you."

"No, play golf." Kathryn's voice was emphatic. "If you break your appointments, people will wonder why and I won't become a source of gossip. People know me here and I don't want them to think that we're, that we're..."

"Sleeping together?"

Kathryn pushed back her chair. The legs made a scrapping sound on the carpet that caused Markham's heart to jump. *She's getting away.* "I'm sorry if I offended you," he said.

"I'm not offended," Kathryn said. "But people talk, don't they?"

"Kathryn…"

"I want to be with you, only not in a crowd. Not so anyone can see."

"I'm open to suggestions."

"Give me your cell phone number. I'll call and tell you where I am."

"When?"

"Whenever. You'll take the call and tell whomever you're with that something requires your immediate attention—that's what doctors do, right? They run off to things that require their immediate attention."

"What if I can't get away?"

"Then that will be the end of that."

Markham slid his business card across the table and the woman slipped it into her bag. "You don't strike me as a woman who plays games, Kathryn," he said.

"Consider it a test of character, Doctor. If you pass, who knows, tomorrow I might let you sit next to me at the seminar for Angiogenesis Inhibitors in Clinical Trials."

"Will we hold hands?"

Kathryn rose from her chair. Her voice was loud and clear. "It was a pleasure to meet you, Doctor."

Markham also stood. He extended his hand. "The pleasure was entirely mine, Doctor," he said.

"You pay for lunch," Kathryn whispered.

Markham watched as she glided out of the restaurant and disappeared into the resort. "That went well," he said to no one in particular.

* * *

Markham signaled for the check. Before it arrived, a tall, thin man dressed like he was going sailing slid into the chair that Kathryn had occupied.

"Who was that?"

"Gee, Stephen. Don't be shy. Have a seat."

"Thank you, I will."

"French fry?"

Markham pushed Kathryn's plate forward. She had eaten the entire teriyaki chicken sandwich she had ordered, yet didn't touch the rest of the meal.

Stephen took three fries and stuffed them into his mouth. He spoke around them. "So, who was that?"

"A doctor from Arizona." Markham couldn't remember where in Arizona; he hadn't been listening that hard when Kathryn told him. "We met at the seminar this morning."

"Why were you having lunch with her?"

Markham stared at the man over the rim of his iced tea. "Just comparing notes," he said.

"Of course," Stephen said. "Silly question. Her legs didn't factor into it at all."

"Stephen..."

"Are you going to tell Susan about her?"

"I don't tell Susan about everyone I have lunch with? How about you?"

That last was less a question than it was an accusation and Stephen knew it. He smiled and ate a few more fries. "I only tell her about the women," he said.

"What's your story, anyway?" Markham asked.

"When Susan learned that we were both attending the same medical convention, she told me to keep an eye on you." As he spoke, he pointed two fingers at his eyes, turned them and pointed the same fingers at Markham's eyes, then repeated the gesture twice more.

"Stop it," Markham said.

"Just looking out for my sister-in-law's interests."

"The fact that your brother is married to Susan's sister does not make you her brother-in-law."

"Honorary brother-in-law."

Markham sighed deeply, dramatically. Stephen snooping around with Kathryn about to call at any minute—*I need this,* he told himself. *I really do.*

"You have no right to interpose yourself into my affairs," he said.

"Affairs. What a splendid way to put it."

"Stephen, I don't know how you got it into your head that I'm cheating on Suz—"

"You've done it before."

The check came. Markham scribbled his room number and name across it and gave it back to the waitress. He waited for her to depart before he spoke.

"That's past history. Susan and I have dealt with the issue and moved on. Not that it's any of your business, but you should do the same."

"You've cheated before. You'll do it again."

"Seriously, Stephen. This jealousy of yours—it's getting old. Susan's married to me. She loves me. I know you have this fantasy of the two of you running away together, but it's not going to happen."

"If you were out of the picture—"

"Not going to happen. If Susan wanted a divorce all she'd have to do is ask. Only she doesn't want a divorce. She didn't want one when things between us were rocky. She won't ask for one now when our marriage is solid."

"Good Catholic girls like Susan don't get divorced."

"Then you're screwed, aren't you, pal?" Markham rose from the table and gave the other man a playful slap on the back. "We need to find you a girl."

Markham shot a half dozen strokes above his handicap, costing him sixty-five dollars and bragging rights to the two doctors and a pharmaceutical rep that completed his foursome. He blamed Kathryn. Every time he tried to visualize his shot, he would see her—usually in various stages of undress. Plus, there were the dozen times he checked his cell phone. Only he didn't use her as an excuse, instead asking the other golfers, "Did I tell you about my sore shoulder?" every time he shanked a ball. Discretion—he figured that was the least he could give her considering what she was about to give him. Besides, he told himself, with Stephen on the prowl he needed to be careful.

After seeing to his clubs, Markham joined his companions on the outdoor patio adjacent to the clubhouse. Three rounds of drinks were consumed, all paid for with the money he had lost. While he joked and drank he thought he saw someone he knew on the short staircase that led from the patio to the rich, green golf course. But the woman's back was turned and she quickly descended the steps before he could get a good look at her. Still, his stomach had an express-elevator-going-down feeling and his face became pale enough that the pharmaceutical rep asked, "Are you feeling all right?"

"Fine," Markham said. "I was just remembering the double-bogey on thirteen." His friends all thought that was pretty funny and a moment later he was laughing, too.

The resort was divided into five parts: the golf course and clubhouse, Heritage Center, marina, casino and resort. From where he sat, Markham could see the roof and upper floors of the latter two buildings. After the third round, the golfers went their separate ways. Markham drifted toward the resort, about a short par four away. As he rounded the clubhouse he heard a voice. "Hello, Doctor." Markham pivoted toward it. Barely ten feet stretched between him and the woman he was sure he had seen on the staircase. Only he was nothing if not adaptable. Instead of showing fear, this time Markham forced a smile.

"Caroline," he said. He moved forward and engulfed her in his arms. She didn't resist the hug, but she didn't hug him back, either. "What are you doing here?"

"My job," Caroline said.

There was rancor in her voice. Markham pretended not to hear it. Seeing her in Northern Minnesota was unexpected, certainly. Still, he was a doctor. He was trained to deal with the unexpected.

"That's right," Markham said. He kissed her cheek. "You work for the drug company."

"You remember."

"Of course, I remember. I only wish I knew you were here, earlier. We could have had lunch. We could have had breakfast." He gave that last word added emphasis. They had had breakfast together once before.

Caroline folded her arms across her chest. "You never called," she said.

"I wanted to. I must have picked up the phone a dozen times."

"But you didn't call."

"How could I, sweetie?" Markham's voice was suddenly filled with regret. "Were we together? Were we ever going to be together? You knew about Susan. You knew…"

Markham turned his head away so the young woman couldn't see the tears that would have been in his eyes if only he had learned how to cry on cue. Something to work on, he told himself. Maybe take an acting class. He felt Caroline's hand on his arm. He covered it with his own hand and gave it a squeeze.

"Is she any better?" Caroline's voice had changed, too. It swung from animosity to commiseration, just as Markham had predicted. Caroline, he knew, could be had.

"No. She had been taking these drugs..."

"Tysabri?" Caroline asked.

"And the Interferons. They don't seem to do much good. She just gets weaker and weaker. She's so tired all the time. She hates it."

"My mother had MS, too."

"You have every right to be angry, Caroline."

"No, no..."

"Only what could I do? Desert my chronically ill wife because I found love with a younger, more beautiful woman? How could I do that to Susan? What kind of man would I be? You wouldn't want to be with a man like that."

"No, you can't leave her."

"And calling you, hearing your voice, knowing we couldn't be together—it was just too much to bear."

Markham hugged the woman's shoulder, buzzed her hair, then abruptly stepped back. "You look terrific," he said. "Just terrific. Are you staying in the resort? Walk back with me."

"I can't."

"Caroline, you have to forgive me"

"Oh, I do, I do forgive you."

Markham sighed with relief, but Caroline heard something else. Her arm hooked around his and she guided him down a path away from both the resort and clubhouse.

"I want to be with you like we were before, I really do," she said. "Only, we need to be careful. They inserted an ethics clause in my contract. If my company discovered I slept with a client, I could lose my job."

"No one else needs to know." Even as he said it, Markham instinctively glanced at his watch. He wondered briefly when Kathryn would call; what would he do if she called right now?

"What do you think?" Caroline asked. They had halted in front of a low-slung cabin that looked from the outside like something early pioneers might have hewed out of the wilderness, provided they had an excellent sense of design.

"Very rustic," Markham said.

"It has three bedrooms, a full kitchen, living room, sauna, wet bar..." It also had a cedar deck that overlooked a pond and they were soon standing on it. "The company turned over all of the bungalows to its reps and left the resort to you guys. I think they wanted to make sure we got a break from each other."

"I wouldn't want a break from you," Markham said. His arm circled the woman's waist and pulled her close. He kissed her mouth. Caroline returned the kiss, but after a moment she broke it off.

"Come inside," she said and pulled him into the bungalow. She closed the door and stood with her back to Markham, gazing out the window at the empty path beyond. "My roommates will be back soon."

Markham rested his hands on the young woman's shoulder. "How soon?" he asked.

Caroline leaned backward against him.

"That time when we were together, I wasn't looking for a fling," Markham said. "When I met you in the bar and we started talking, I thought, hey, here's an interesting, intelligent woman. We seemed to have so much in common. We even have the same favorite song. What were the odds of that?"

"Someone To Watch Over Me," Caroline said.

Markham was glad she remembered the title; he hadn't. His hands slid slowly down her bare arms, his fingertips gently caressed her flesh. She had goosebumps.

"I didn't think about us being together until we were on the elevator and I asked you what floor," Markham said.

"And I said five."

"And I was on eight."

"And the doors opened at five."

"And you didn't get off."

"Oh, God."

Caroline spun in Markham's arms and kissed him hard on the mouth. Markham was about to ask which of the three bedrooms belonged to her when Caroline pushed him away.

"Not now," she said. "Later. Tell me your room number and I'll meet you later."

Only later had been reserved for Kathryn.

"I... we'll see," Markham said.

The expression his remark put on Caroline's face frightened him. He actually took two steps backward.

"Why won't you tell me?" she said. "Are you seeing someone else? You are, aren't you? You're seeing someone else."

Just like that, Markham was tap-dancing on the edge of a scalpel. He knew Caroline would never confess to Susan that she was banging her husband.

But tell her that someone else was sleeping with him—well, why wouldn't she? Women scorned, they need to stick together, don't they?

"Of course I not seeing anyone else," he said.

"You are."

The last time Markham had heard a voice sound that accusatory was years ago in an emergency room when a mother confronted the teenager who had just whacked her daughter with a car.

"Listen to me, Caroline."

"Damn you."

Caroline took three quick steps and pushed violently against Markham's chest. The momentum forced him backward. She pushed him again, but this time she didn't have a running start and he held his ground. When she attempted to pound his chest with clenched fists, he caught both of her wrists and pulled her close.

"Stop it," he snarled. "There are two women in my life. There's Susan and then there's you. No one else. Now stop it."

"I just want to be with you."

"I want to be with you, too. But I have a brother-in-law here who's been watching me and I have to be careful."

"A brother-in-law? At the resort?"

"Yes."

Caroline covered her mouth with her hand. "Oh, God, I'm so sorry," she said. "I thought... oh, God."

Markham wrapped her in his arms. "It's okay, it's all right," he told her.

"I thought..."

"I don't blame you."

Markham sighed. Another bullet dodged, he told himself. He stole a look at his watch. Kathryn was going to call at any moment and if Caroline saw them together... He had a thought that made him smile.

"Have dinner with me tonight," he said.

"What about your brother-in-law?"

"We'll ask him to join us."

Caroline seemed terrified by the prospect. "Your brother-in-law?"

"That's kind of a joke, we're not really related. But here's the thing—he's a doctor and I'm a doctor and you're a rep. Why wouldn't we get together for dinner? What could be more innocent? You can even make it a business dinner; give us your sales pitch." And pay the check, Markham thought but didn't say. "Afterwards," Caroline brightened at the word, "we'll go to the casino. And then, who knows?"

"I always lose when I gamble," Caroline said.

"Not me."

Dr. Brookline was an old man and some on his staff—including Markham—actively pushed for his retirement. Even now he sat at a glass table on the resort's back patio, studying the handouts the pharmaceutical companies distributed because he was terrified that the advances in medicine would pass him by. Markham tried to avoid him, only Brookline saw him before he could escape.

"Good afternoon, Doctor," Brookline said. He gestured for Markham to sit. Markham sat.

"Good afternoon, Doctor," Markham replied.

"How have you been spending your day?"

"I just finished playing eighteen holes with…"

"I meant which seminars did you attend."

"Of course." Markham gave him a quick recap and Brookline nodded. He hummed a few times, but Markham didn't know if that meant he was pleased or not.

"You're a very good physician," Brookline said.

"Thank you, Doctor."

"There have been suggestions that it was time I retired."

"No."

"Some members of the board have indicated that they expect you to replace me."

"No one could replace you."

"Thank you for that, Doctor. Still, perhaps it is time. One is not getting any younger. The question is, are you ready to step into my shoes? I'll be frank, Doctor. There have been times when you have impressed me with, what shall I call it, your lack of judgment."

"Sir?"

"I am referring solely to your judgment outside the hospital. One hears rumors."

"I don't know how to respond to that, Doctor. I assure you that I have always tried to behave with the utmost caution in my personal affairs."

Brookline hummed some more.

"It is a discussion for a different time and place," he said. "We'll talk again when we return home."

With that, the old man went back to his handouts. Markham stood slowly. He knew when he had been dismissed.

"Sir," he said. "I am having dinner with Dr. Krueger and a rep from a pharmaceutical company. Perhaps you'd care to join us?"

"Thank you, Doctor, I already have plans. Dr. Krueger, you say? A steady hand. I am gratified to see you spending time with him."

Oh brother, Markham thought.

Markham couldn't believe it was possible. Caroline actually seemed to like the sniveling little creep. The way they connected, it was as if they had known each other for years. She laughed at Stephen's jokes and when she laughed, she would touch his arm and he would blush, actually blush, like a teenager on a first date. What comedy, Markham thought. Especially when they wrestled over the check. Caroline told Stephen that she would put it on her expense account, but if he really felt guilty about it, he could teach her how to play blackjack. "I'm terrible at cards," she said. Still, it gave Markham another idea.

Before they left the restaurant, Caroline stopped at the restroom. While they waited, Markham punched Stephen in the shoulder. "You dawg," he said. "I didn't think you had it in you."

Stephen rubbed the spot where he had been hit. "What?"

"Like you don't know. 'Oh, please, Stephen. Can you teach me to play blackjack? I'm terrible at cards.'"

Stephen smiled sheepishly.

"You realize of course, that these reps have ethics clauses in their contracts," Markham said. "They're forbidden to sleep with clients."

"Really?" Stephen said. "Are you sure?"

Markham put his arm around Stephen's shoulder. "Don't worry about it. Rules are made to be broken, aren't they?"

Caroline and Stephen kept losing no matter how much they tried to help each other. Yet, neither of them seemed to care and for a moment, Markham felt a slight pang of jealousy. It disappeared when the cell phone attached to his belt started vibrating.

"Yes," he said into the phone.

"You are such a slut," Kathryn's voice said.

"Yes, this is Doctor Markham."

"You slept with her, didn't you?"

Markham slid his hand over the cell. "Excuse me," he told his companions and backed away from the blackjack table. Caroline watched him for a moment, then returned to her cards.

"What are you talking about?" Markham asked

"I've been watching you. The way you touch her of so casually when you're sure no one else will notice. It's so obvious."

"Is it?"

Kathryn laughed. "You should see your face," she said.

"What's wrong with my face?"

"From here it looks like you're experiencing an aneurysm."

"Where are you?" Markham spun in a slow, tight circle, searching for the woman.

"You'll see me soon enough," she said.

"Where?"

"The marina. There's a white cabin cruiser docked at the end of the middle pier. It's called *Miss Behavin'*. Meet me there in ten minutes. Don't let anyone see you. Promise."

Sex in a boat, that would be new, Markham thought. "I promise," he said.

"I have a sheer black negligee," Kathryn said. "Only it's such a warm night, I might not be wearing it by the time you arrive."

Markham deactivated the cell and reattached it to his belt. He returned to the blackjack table, stopping behind Caroline and Stephen. He placed a hand on each of their backs.

"Play my chips for me," he said. "I need to take care of something."

"You're leaving?" Caroline asked.

"No rest for the wicked," Markham said.

"Is it serious?" Stephen asked.

Markham wagged his hand. "I don't know yet. It could be. Caroline..." Markham wrapped his arms around her, hugged her tight and said loudly, "It was a pleasure meeting you. Let's do it again." Into her ear he whispered, "I'll call." He didn't hug Stephen, but Markham shook his hand and whispered into his ear as well. "Break the rules."

He pulled back and looked him in the eye. "You know what I'm saying?"

"I know," Stephen said.

The marina lay on the far side of the resort. To reach it, Markham had to leave the casino, follow a long asphalt path to the resort itself, pass through the resort to the patio in back, pick up the asphalt path again and follow it between the 11th and 12th holes of the golf course to the lake. He was tempted to run, only he didn't want to be tired and sweaty when he met Kathryn.

It's too bad about Caroline, he told himself. But if she slept with Stephen, it would afford him an excuse to break it off completely with her. If she complained, he'd tell her, "I used Stephen to see if you were faithful and you failed the test. Pity."

As he cut through the resort's opulent lobby, Markham was stopped by a man calling his name. Brookline was sitting in a stuffed forest-green chair and examining a medical journal, his black-rimming reading glasses perched on the tip of his nose.

"Calling it a night so soon, Dr. Markham?"

Why do these things keep happening to me? Markham's inner voice shouted.

"Good evening, Doctor," he said. "Yes. Early to bed early to rise."

"I am gladdened to see it."

"I'm not much of a gambler. Besides, there's a seminar early tomorrow morning."

"Quite so," said Brookline. "I was thinking of

turning in myself. But," he gestured with his ancient hand toward the bar, "perhaps one might interest you in a nightcap."

"Thank you, Doctor. But I promised I'd call Susan."

"Of course." Brookline stood, yawned, stretched, and said, "I'll go up with you."

Markham and Dr. Brookline rode the elevator together—they were on the same floor. With his luck, Markham figured it couldn't be any other way. Brookline walked slowly along the corridor and Markham forced himself to keep pace. Markham came to his door first.

"Perhaps we can have breakfast together before the seminar," Brookline said.

"I'd like that very much, sir," Markham said.

"I'll call for you."

"I'll be waiting."

Markham opened his door, went into the room, closed his door, took his phone off the hook, sat on the wine-colored love seat, counted two hundred ten seconds by his watch, opened the door, hung a Do Not Disturb sign on the knob and scrambled down the emergency staircase.

Lake Vermillion shimmered in the moonlight. It had twelve hundred miles of shoreline and three hundred sixty-five islands and Markham thought it would be great fun to take the boat and Kathryn and explore some of those islands. There were three piers jutting into the lake. Markham took the center one. Markham could hear only soft waves lapping gently at the hulls of the boats moored in the slips and the muffled sound of his footsteps on the wooden planks. He walked past fishing boats, pontoons, tour boats and an assortment of larger craft, some owned by guests, others for rent. At the end of the pier he found a white, thirty-foot cabin cruiser. The name *Miss Behavin'* was stenciled on her bow and stern.

"Ahoy."

Kathryn's voice answered from the interior of the boat. "Dr. Markham?"

"Yes."

"Are you alone?"

"Yes."

"Did anyone see you? Does anyone know you're here?"

"Not a soul."

"Come aboard."

Markham stepped onto the deck of the boat and followed Kathryn's voice into the cabin. The moonlight that flooded through the narrow windows let him see the outline of furniture. Kathryn slid out of a shadow. She was naked.

"I like your outfit," Markham said, although he would have been happier if the lights were on and he could see more than her shape.

Kathryn stepped forward. Her face slipped from shadow to light and into shadow again. She was grinning. Once again Markham wished that the lights were on. He reached for her, rested his hands on the points of her bare shoulder. He liked the way her warm flesh felt beneath his fingertips. His arms slipped around her and he pull her against him.

"I am so lucky that you sat in my row at the seminar," he said.

"Luck had nothing to do with it."

"What do you mean?"

"I have a message from your wife."

"My wife?"

"Susan says, 'You failed the test.'"

"What?"

Markham felt the eleven-blade scalpel slice through the intercostal muscles between the fourth and fifth ribs and penetrate the left atrium of his heart. He found Kathryn's face in the darkness.

"Doctor," he said, as he collapsed to the floor.

But of course, she wasn't a doctor.

Author's Note: This story is also inspired by true events. A St. Paul man sued his friend claiming that the friend stole the design for his headstone. Some things you just can't make up.

Last Laugh

The old man kept repeating himself in different tones of voice and at different volumes, yet still he couldn't make the youngster understand him.

"It's my design," he said.

"It's not," the young man said.

The old man pointed at his photograph. "Look it," he said. "It's the same black marble. It's the same shape and size. It has the same drawing etched into the stone—a pastoral scene with a path leading to a cloud-draped sunset. Here's the plank fence, here's the maple tree, here's the two deer."

"Mr. Garber," the young man said. "I admit the tombstones are similar in appearance. However, if you look closely, you'll see that ours is ten percent larger. As for the etching, in our design we have a road leading to the horizon, not a path, and it follows a picket fence, not a plank fence. We incorporated a fir tree, not a maple, and as for the deer—you have a buck and a doe while we have a buck and a fawn."

"What about the inscription?" Garber said.

"All I seek, the heaven above and the road below me," the young man read. "It's a common slogan. Shakespeare, I believe."

"It's from Robert Louis Stevenson."

Garber felt his granddaughter's hand tighten on his forearm; saw the concern in her face. He had seen the look many times since his last doctor's appointment. He patted Johanna's hand and gave her a smile in return.

"I don't know why I'm upset," he said. "Put the gravestones side-by-side and anyone can see it's like comparing apples to apples."

"Sir," the young man said. "The Studders Monument Company is not in the habit of pilfering designs. As I explained, our client Mr. Tinklenberg brought a sketch to us and requested that we duplicate it, and so we did..."

"He stole it from me," Garber said.

"Sir, if you believe your copyright has been infringed upon, you have every right to take legal action. I will refer your complaint to our legal department and we will let the courts sort it out."

"How long do you think that'll take? I'd be dead and buried before it went to trial."

The young man leaned back in his chair. "Certainly we would hope not," he said.

Once outside, Johanna gave Garber an arm to lean on as they descended the concrete stairs leading to the mortuary's parking lot. Garber shrugged it off and took her hand, instead.

"Sugar, I'm not an invalid," he said.

"Grandpa, the doctors said—"

"The doctors said..."

Garber sighed like it was a subject he had tired of long ago. Still, he saw the anxiety in Johanna's eyes, so he grinned and rapped his chest with his fist just like Johnny Weissmuller did in all those *Tarzan* movies. It sent a sudden and unexpected shock of pain through his bones; he winced and coughed, and then added a brilliant smile and pretended to stagger so Johanna would think it was a joke.

"I've lived a lot of years," he said. "For the most part I've had a crackerjack of a time. The docs wanna inject me with their drugs and douse me with their radiation but what's that gonna get me? Another year at the most. A bad year. I'd rather take the three months and go out with a little style." He glanced about like he was suddenly afraid the cops were listening and his voice dropped a few octaves. "Especially, if you score some of that medicinal marijuana you promised me."

Johanna chuckled just as he hoped she would. Garber brought Johanna's hand to his lips and kissed her knuckle.

"In the meantime," he said, "I have to figure out what to do about Tinklenberg."

"Who is he?" Johanna said.

"Just a guy from the neighborhood. Vern Tinklenberg. He moved in when we were kids and he didn't know anybody. He wanted to fit in, so he started copying everything I did. I played ball, so he played ball. I played hockey, so he played hockey. I'd get in trouble at school and sure as hell, the next thing he'd be in trouble at school. It got to be a habit with him. I remember the morning after the

Japs bombed Pearl Harbor, I was first in line to join the army; didn't even tell my mom until afterward. Vern heard about it so he enlisted the next day; yet he's talked it up ever since like he was the first in line. He'd tell stories about the war, too. Talk about things that happened to me, to others, like they happened to him. I was shelled on, mortared on, rained on, snowed on, strafed, machine-gunned, bombed, and shot at all the way from Normandy to the Rhine. Meanwhile, Vern was in San Antonio eating barbecue. Man didn't even get to Europe until April '45 and by then it was all over but the shouting. Only to hear Vern talk about it, you'd think he was George friggin' Patton and Audie Murphy rolled into one. Didn't stop there, neither. No, sir. I'd see him around afterward and it was always how big is your house, mine is bigger; what car do you drive, mine is newer; how much money do you make, I make more; how many kids do you have, three? I got four. Now this. Pretty low, even for him."

"Why would he steal your tombstone?" Johanna said. "Why now? You don't think...?"

Johanna hesitated, frightened by the words that had formed in her head. Garber heard them even though they went unspoken.

"Sugar, only the good die young," he said. "Pricks like Vern Tinklenberg, they live forever. Although..."

Garber halted in the middle of the parking lot; Johanna was three steps past before she realized it and turned to face him.

"If he did die first, people would think I copied his crummy memorial instead of the other way 'round," Garber said. "Course, if he died soon enough, I'd still have time to build a monument that would make his look like a tar-paper shack on a dirt road."

They blocked off both ends of the avenue where Garber had grown up with huge sawhorses painted white with orange stripes. There was a sign from the city on the barricades—No Thru Traffic—and another from the neighborhood—Block Party 6—10:30 PM.

Garber sat with Johanna at one of the many picnic tables that had been dragged into the street. He had been drinking ice cold beer and eating flame-grilled chicken and corn-on-the-cob dipped in sweet butter and he thought, if this turned out to be his last meal, it wasn't too shabby. Johanna had tried to dissuade him from coming. She sensed her grandfather's excruciating pain even if he refused to acknowledge it. Yet Garber couldn't resist the chance to see the old neighborhood one last time and those few childhood friends that were still alive and kicking. Besides there was a band and Garber had always loved to dance. Granted, the band wasn't very good and mostly they played Golden Oldies that were nowhere near as aged as the songs that he considered golden, but he could dance to anything.

At first Johanna had refused to dance with him, insisting instead that he sit and rest. She stepped in only after watching Garber shake and shimmy and twist with the forty-year-old babe that was currently living next to the house where he grew up, and then with the thirty-year-old babe who now lived across the street—lately Garber considered nearly every woman he met to be a babe.

"You have moves," Garber told her.

"I inherited them from you," Johanna said.

"Nah, Sugar, you got 'em from your grandmother. My, how that woman could dance. Oww!"

It pleased Johanna that Garber was having fun. Yet at the same time it distressed her to see him pressing his hand against the small of his back beneath his cotton sports jacket as if there was something there that required constant attention. He had become so old and so thin in just a few weeks. She held him close as the rock band slowed into *Fools Rush In (Where Angels Fear To Tread)*, a 1940's ballad that Ricky Nelson turned into a Top 40 rock & roll hit twenty-five years later. Garber sang the words sweet and low into her ear. When he stopped abruptly, Johanna looked into his face, expecting the worst. Garber's eyes had narrowed, not with pain, but with anger. She followed his gaze across the makeshift dance floor to where the picnic tables had been set up. A man close to Garber's age was holding court, waving his arms as he told a story.

"Vern Tinklenberg," Garber said. "I knew he'd be here."

"I wish he hadn't come," Johanna said.

"You know what, Sugar? Me, too."

Garber moved up behind Tinklenberg and listened to him tell his tale. He knew the story well.

"They used to have ski jumping over at Como Park," Tinklenberg said. "This was back in the thirties, early forties. I remember this one time, a guy dared me to go down the jump. Double-dared me. You know how kids are. I couldn't back away from a double-dare. So I climbed the ramp with my toboggan—I had this long, wooden toboggan. I went down the jump, flew off the bottom. Suddenly, I'm airborne. Seemed like I was up there forever, holding on to the toboggan for dear life. It was actually kinda fun for about five seconds. Then I came down, hit the hill. Hard. Next thing I know, I'm spread-eagle over the hood of some guy's car, my toboggan smashed to bits, and the guy's asking if I'm all right. He wanted to take me to the hospital, only I'm more afraid of my mother than I was of being hurt. So I go home, make up a story about the toboggan getting run over by a car, never told my mother anything until three days later when they took me to the hospital cuz I had three broken ribs and one of them punctured my lung. I'll tell you, if I wasn't already in the hospital, that's where she would have put me."

Tinklenberg's audience laughed politely, Garber included. He moved out from behind him.

"That's a good story, Vern," Garber said. "Funny."

Tinklenberg smiled in recognition. "Hi, Al." He stopped smiling.

"'Cept it didn't happen to you," Garber said. "It happened to Bob Foley. I know cuz I was the one who double-dared him."

"What are you talking about, Al?"

Garber circled Tinklenberg, putting a worn wooden picnic table between them.

"You're a fraud," he said. "A phony. You've never done anything in your life worth talkin' about so you tell other people's stories, pretending they're all about you."

"That's B.S." Tinklenberg turned to his audience. "Al's always been jealous. Ever since we were kids. Cuz I was always better than him."

"Who are you kidding?" Garber said. "You've never been better than me at anything. Ever."

"I hit more home runs than you. I scored more goals, killed more Nazis, made more money; my wife was prettier."

"Lies, lies, lies. Is that how you wanna go out? Rowing across the River Styx in a boat of lies?" Garber found his granddaughter and smiled at her. "Like that, Sugar? River Styx?" He turned back to his adversary. "You were always second best, Vern. At least that's what your wife told me. You know what I'm talking about."

"You sonuvabitch," Tinklenberg said. "Ruth would never have had anything to do with you."

Garber held his hands away from his body, palms up.

"A gentleman never tells," he said.

He found Johanna again and gave her a wink and Johanna wondered if Garber really did sleep with Tinklenberg's wife or if he was just needling him.

"You're a liar," Tinklenberg shouted.

"I'm a liar? Look up the word in the dictionary, pal, and there's your photo, both front and profile like the way the cops take 'em."

Tinklenberg made a move as if he was about to go over the picnic table for Garber. But Garber calmly held his ground. He reached behind him underneath the sports jacket and produced a gun. There was a collected gasp from the neighbors who had gathered round to watch the confrontation; more than one reached for a cell phone. Garber held up the gun for everyone to see.

"Know what this is?" he said.

"It's a Luger," Tinklenberg said.

"That's what we call it. The Krauts call it *Pistolen-08.* "

"Big deal. I have one just like it."

"Except I took mine off a German officer at the Remagen Bridge. You paid fifty bucks for yours in London."

"I got mine off a prisoner."

"You bought it from Jack Finnegan. He told me." Garber smiled some more. "Second best again, Vern."

He leveled the gun on Tinklenberg's chest.

"Grandpa," Johanna called.

Garber waved her away with his free hand.

"Sugar, please," he said. "I'm trying to make a point."

"Don't, Al, please, you can't," Tinklenberg said. "You can't—please—don't shoot me."

"Why not? I won't live long enough to go to trial for it, much less prison."

"Al."

"You stole my tombstone, Vern. Did you think I wouldn't find out? You stole it just like you've stolen my stories and took them for your own, stories about my life and the lives of a lot of other men better than you. Well, why not? Why not steal my tombstone? Your whole life you've been chasing after me—hell, you haven't had a life. You've been too busy living mine. Didn't do nearly as good a job, either. Take the tombstone. What do you think, people are going to point at it and say 'Tinklenberg, what a man, his monument is ten percent bigger than Al Garber's?' That ain't gonna happen. You know what's gonna happen? They're going to point and say, 'It's bigger than Al's monument, but not nearly as good. It's second best.' Just like the life you've lived."

Garber thumbed back the hammer on the Pistolen-08 and extended his arm.

"No, Al." Tinklenberg brought both his hands up to defend his face. He screamed. "No."

Several neighbors joined in.

"No."

Garber squeezed the trigger.

Click.

There was a moment of perfect silence while dozens of ears strained to hear the sharp snap of a gunshot. When it didn't come, the silence slowly filled with the distant sound of a police siren coming closer, the shouts of neighbors, and with Garber's loud, unrestrained laughter.

"Oh, you should see your face," he said.

Tinklenberg's eyes were wet with tears; a stain spread along his pants from his crotch and down his leg. He cursed Garber but there was no energy in it.

"Hey, I just did you a favor, Vern. Now you have a story to tell that really is your own."

Garber found his granddaughter and smiled.

"Remember, Sugar," he said. "Tombstones, they don't matter all that much. I mean, who gives a crap, really? What matters, is that you live well and have a little fun. Otherwise, what's the point?"

He laughed some more. Laughed as he dropped the unloaded Pistolen-08 into his pocket. Laughed as he made his way back to the dance floor. With a little luck, he figured he could get in a few more dances before it was time to go.

Author's Note: This story came to me while I was having lunch in a small town along the Mississippi River with my wife. It was originally titled Meg and Josie's Hotel, Restaurant and Bar Across From Karla's Kut and Kurl in Alma, Wisconsin. *But cooler heads prevailed.*

Obsessive Behavior

They tossed my room after the fifth day. Actually, Josie searched it while Meg banged my brains out in her living quarters in the back of the hotel. I would have preferred Josie. Meg had bluer eyes, blonder hair and bigger breasts, but the lovely, doe-eyed Josie gave off a girl-next-door vibe that more than once made me reconsider my life choices. It was easy to see why Johnny the Boy Scalise had fallen for her, why he had trusted her with the combination to his safe.

Josie hadn't found anything in my room. That's because I had brought nothing that would have identified me as a PI; I didn't even bring my guns. Still, I had taken a chance letting Meg seduce me. Josie was sharp—all three of them were sharp—yet they lacked experience, otherwise they would have known that the smart move was to go for the cell phone in the pocket of my sports jacket that Meg had stripped off before leading me to her bedroom. They would have seen all those numbers in the call log with the 312 prefix for Chicago and they would have been frightened. If they had re-dialed the last

139

number I had called, they would have been have been frightened even more.

I didn't want the girls to be frightened. I wanted them relaxed, calm. Only Johnny the Boy had crossed me up. He had told me to sit on the girls until he arrived. That was six days ago and still no sign of him. You simply cannot hang out for that long at Meg and Josie's Hotel, Restaurant and Bar—that's its actual name—without making people suspicious. The joint was located in Alma, Wisconsin, a 19th Century-style European village filled with inns, bed and breakfasts, art galleries, gift shops and restaurants that was perched on a narrow strip of land between the Mississippi River and a five hundred-foot-high limestone bluff. It catered to tourists chasing walleye or the fall colors, birders attracted by the nesting grounds of bald eagles and rail buffs enticed by the thirty trains that passed through the town each day. Yet while many people came and went, as a rule they didn't linger for long. But still there I was after nearly a week, keeping to myself and neither fishing, birding nor trainspotting. Of course, the girls were alarmed. I would have been alarmed, too. Especially if I was on the lam with three point two million of a gangster's ill-gotten dollars.

I liked the girls very much, had liked them even before I met them. Johnny had called them whores, skanks, bitches. They weren't. They were professional women, graduates of Northwestern University; they could speak five foreign languages between them. Brenda worked in public relations, Cassidy was an economist and Linda was trying to parlay an art history degree into a career in high fashion as a hair stylist. Just about everyone I met while searching for them spoke of their kindness, their generosity, their unbridled sense of fun. Their only crime, it seemed, was falling in with the wrong crowd.

Brenda had taken up with Johnny the Boy, Cassidy with his Number One henchman, and the third—Linda—she was their roommate. Things went from bad to worse almost immediately. Cassidy was sent to the emergency room when the henchman lost fifty large betting on the Bears in the 2006 Super Bowl—he had to take his frustration out on someone. The incident so appalled Brenda that she broke it off with Johnny. At least she tried to. Johnny refused to take no for an answer, ignoring the restraining order forbidding him to go anyway near Brenda, threatening her friends with rape and murder if she didn't wise up and scaring off every lawyer that tried to come to her rescue.

This lasted for nearly a year. Then poof, the girls were gone. The cops couldn't find them, although they didn't look very hard, and neither could Johnny. It became apparent that the girls were living under fake IDs that were as solid as anything provided by the U. S. Marshall's Witness Security Program because three years of relentless effort by some very good bounty hunters couldn't put a dent in them.

To pull off a magic act like that, they would have needed help. So I went to a guy I knew who specialized in disappearances. Johnny's boys had interrogated him, too, and got nothing, but he owed me a favor and to pay it off he told me a story. It was about three beautiful princesses who had begged—literally begged—a good wizard a traveling bard had spoken about to help them escape from an evil monster. The wizard liked the princesses very much, plus it didn't hurt that they had a boatload of treasure. The wizard hid them in the forest until he was able to conjure a spell that rendered the princesses invisible. It was the finest work he had ever done—his masterpiece—and he boasted that no one would ever find and hurt the princesses again.

Which was good enough for me. Except Johnny the Boy started demanding results. I explained that while I had great faith in my craft, it was unlikely I could do in a short time what others couldn't accomplish over a period of years and he should forget the whole thing. Johnny didn't see it that way.

"They claim you can find anybody," he said.

"That's not entirely true."

"It better be."

Johnny the Boy suggested that I try harder and then started listing the names of family members and friends that might suffer due to my lack of success. I didn't think for a moment that he was bluffing. I understood Johnny's obsession. If it should become known that three girls fresh out of college had ripped him off and gotten away with it, well, a lot of Johnny Boy's rivals would look upon it as a sign of weakness, something you just didn't show in his line of work. Already there were rumors that Tony the Ant and Jimmy Legs were preparing to move on him, which was why Johnny the Boy so rarely left the fortress he had built for himself on Lake Michigan.

I didn't like it, but I went back to work in earnest, accumulating every piece of information about the girls that I could. See, the key to finding someone who is hiding in plain sight is the past. People are creatures of habit. After spending a lifetime doing a specific thing in a certain way, it becomes extremely difficult, if not impossible, to change. A fugitive who was an accountant, goes back to being an accountant; a used car salesman might give up cars, but odds are he'll sell something else. The girls had been footloose and fancy free for over three years now. Possibly they were sliding back into their old lives, whether they had meant to or not. Possibly they were making mistakes.

I catalogued the magazines the girls had subscribed to and bought the subscription lists to all of them. I compiled the names and addresses of the business organizations they had joined and secured a list of members. I examined the membership directories and subscription lists of every public-relations-related association and newsletter I could find. I searched the motor vehicle licenses and registrations of forty-nine states and the criminal records of every county in all fifty states. I hired an information broker and had her hunt through bank accounts that had been opened within the past three years. I paid an IRS agent under the table to check on any female who was either depositing large sums of money in an account on a regular basis or passing large sums from one account to another. The most time consuming thing I did was look up the names of every woman between the ages of twenty and thirty who was issued a license by a State Board of Cosmetology somewhere in the U. S. in the past three years. Then I cross-referenced it all. It took me three months to find Karla's Kut & Kurl, opened just nine months earlier in Alma. Once I had that, it took three hours to find Meg and Josie's Hotel, Restaurant and Bar.

I drove out there. I popped into Karla's Kut & Kurl for a haircut. I recognized Linda instantly. She was all sweetness and light and she gave me the best haircut I ever had. While she was working a young woman entered the shop. With tears in her eyes she hugged Karla, thanked for profusely and told her that she was the kindest person ever. After the woman left I asked Karla what it was all about.

"She had a problem," Karla said. "I helped. No biggie."

I pressed but Karla wouldn't give me any more. I liked her for that.

After the haircut, she told me if I was looking for a meal or place to hang my hat, I couldn't do any better than Meg and Josie's place across the street. She leaned in and whispered.

"We're friends, so if you tell them I sent you they'll treat you just as shabbily as they do me."

The hotel registration desk was on the left as you entered the front door; the bar and restaurant were on the right. The restaurant had a nice lunch-hour trade; I didn't see a single empty table. Brenda met me at the door with a menu in her hand.

"I'm Josie," she said. "Can I help you?"

"Karla sent me," I said.

Josie hooked an arm under mine.

"Would you like to sit at the bar?" she asked.

She led me there before I could reply. She sat me on a stool and waved over the woman who was tending bar. Cassidy smiled as brightly as Brenda.

"Meg," Josie said. "This young man is a friend of Karla's."

"Oh," Meg said. "Are you married?"

"No, I'm not," I said.

"Neither is Karla."

For the next ninety minutes, they joked with me as if I was someone they were trying to set up with their little sister. That and the meal made it the most enjoyable lunch I could remember.

All during the drive back to Chicago I tried to think of how to avoid telling Johnny the Boy what I knew. There was no way. I liked the girls very much, but I had family and friends that I liked more. I told him everything. He asked about his money.

"They own a hotel," I said. "They own a hair salon. I don't know anything beyond that."

Johnny's henchman grinned.

"They'll tell us before we're done with them," he said.

I didn't like the implication, but what could I do?

Johnny the Boy gave me fifty grand in an envelope. That in itself made me nervous. Johnny wasn't the kind to give away fifty-K unless he intended to take it back. He then said he would pay me another ten large to go back to Alma and watch the girls until he arrived. It wasn't a request and I didn't take it as such. I drove back that night, settling into a room third floor front. The stretch of the Great River Road that passed through Alma was designated a National Scenic Byway, although there wasn't much to see from my window. Just the river, railroad tracks, a boat ramp, Lock and Dam Number Four and directly across from the hotel, the neon lights of Karla's Kut & Kurl. But that's where I spent most of my time, watching, waiting.

The rest I spent in the restaurant and bar. I came to know the girls quite well, mostly from customers—they didn't talk much about themselves. My favorite story was about how they had organized protests to keep the mayor from awarding the snowplowing contract to his brother-in-law and then, two weeks later when they learned the mayor's wife was diagnosed with breast cancer, hosted a fund-raiser to help pay her medical bills.

It was about eleven thirty on the evening of the sixth day when they called me out. The bar was empty—there wasn't much nightlife in Alma during the middle of the week. I was sitting at the bar nursing a draft. Meg stood on the other side, a bar towel in her hand. Josie was still my favorite, but Meg had risen considerably in my estimation since the evening before. Josie sat on my right, Karla on my left.

"Who are you?" Karla asked.

"Kent Kramer," I said

"We know that," Josie said. "Why are you here?"

I didn't answer.

"You know who we are, don't you?" Meg said.

"I know who you are. I just don't know what names to call you."

"Darn it," Karla said.

"Does Johnny Scalise know?" Meg said.

"Yes."

"I knew it," Josie said. "I knew this day would come."

"Darn it," Karla said again.

Josie rested her head on the top of the bar.

"Now what?" she said.

As if on cue a man wearing a black suit, black shirt and black tie entered the bar. He paused at the entrance, found a table near the door and sat down facing us. All of us watched him intently. Karla gasped. Josie reached out and grabbed my arm. Meg had the presence of mind to circle the bar and walk up to his table.

"Good evening," she said. "May I get you something?"

"Seven and seven," the man answered.

Meg returned to the bar, mixed the drink and served it to the man.

"Thank you," he said.

We all watched him sipping the drink. He pretended not to notice. ESPN was on the monitor above the bar and he fixed his gaze on it and did not look away.

"What should we do?" Karla asked.

"Wait," I said.

I took a long pull of the beer. Josie became agitated.

"I'm not waiting," she said.

I took her hand.

"Please," I said. "Wait."

ESPN went through two commercial cycles while we waited. Finally, we all heard the ring of a cell phone. The man reached into his pocket, took it out and answered it.

"Yeah," he said. He paused. "All right."

He returned the phone to his pocket even as he rose from the chair. He walked across the bar. As he approached, he slid his hand under his suit jacket. Karla gasped again. The man smiled at her reaction. He produced an envelope from his inside pocket.

"You Kramer?" he asked.

I nodded. He set the envelope on the bar in front of me.

"Compliments of Jimmy Legs," he said.

I took the envelope and put it in my own pocket. I didn't open it; I didn't count the money that I knew was inside.

"Everything all right?" I asked.

"All right for us, not so much for Johnny the Boy," he answered.

"What took so long?"

"Johnny got it into his head that it was unsafe to leave his place in Chicago. Took a lot to lure him out. If he hadn't known about the ladies here, if he hadn't been so obsessed…"

The man nodded his head at the girls and left the bar.

It took a few moments before the four of us started breathing again.

"What just happened?" Josie asked.

I got up from the bar and turned toward the three girls.

"You can probably go home now if you want to. Questions will be asked, but..." I raised the palms of my hands upward and shrugged. Afterward I gave the place a parting glance. "I really like it here."

I moved to the door. Josie intercepted me. Her dark eyes cut off a chunk of my heart; I could feel her tucking it away in her pocket. She hugged me and kissed my cheek and said thank you.

I left and I never went back, although I've thought about it often.

Author's Note: My pal, thriller-writer Anne Frasier (aka romance-novelist Theresa Weir), asked me to contribute a story to a Halloween anthology she was editing. I'm not entirely sure I believe in ghosts, but plenty of people do. Who knows, though? Maybe, maybe... ah ha ha ha ha ha...

Time of Death

A small brick building, one story high and less than thirty feet across crouched in the middle of the block. It was the police station, although there was no sign that said so. A uniformed sergeant sat behind an old, battered desk. As far as Logan could tell, he was the only man in the station house.

"He'p ya?" the sergeant said.

Logan flashed his ID.

"Yeah, the chief said you'd be around," the sergeant said. "Come to look at our killer, did you?"

"That's right."

"Pretty little thing. Hard to believe she slashed her boyfriend's throat. 'Course, she denies it."

"I bet she does," Logan said.

"I gotta tell ya..." The sergeant grunted as he lifted his enormous frame from the chair and circled the desk. "I 'spect you see this sorta thing all the time, but a small town like this one, I gotta tell ya, it's the biggest thing ever happened here. Well, second biggest thing. I can understand why the chief would call in you big-city boys."

The sergeant led Logan to the back of the building. There was a heavy metal door with a small window. The window was made of thick glass crisscrossed with iron threads. Logan looked through the glass. The girl was sitting on the edge of a narrow cot attached to the wall, her head in her hands.

"There she is," the sergeant said. He fitted a key into the lock and gave it a turn. The door swung open. "Want I should stay?"

"That won't be necessary," Logan said. "But I'm expecting a report from the medical examiner. Let me know when it arrives."

"You got it."

Logan stepped into the cell. The sergeant closed the door and locked him in.

"Laurel Clark," he said.

The girl looked up. Her eyes were swollen and her cheeks were puffy from crying. She wore her hair in a ponytail tied with a red ribbon but the ribbon had become loose and Logan figured a firm head shake would send it flying. She rubbed her eyes with the back of her hands and looked up again. Logan decided that there was something extraordinarily touching about her, but quickly shook the thought from his head. You know better than that, he told himself.

He let her look at his badge and identification.

"My name is Logan. I'm with the Minnesota Bureau of Criminal Apprehension."

"It's all my fault," she said.

"Ms. Clark, have you been informed of your rights?"

152

She said she had, but he read them to her again anyway. He asked how old she was.

"Nineteen," she said. Which made her a legal adult. Which meant he did not have to inform her parents before questioning her. If she had said she was sixteen, Logan would have believed her.

"Will you answer some questions for me?" he asked.

"Sure."

"You don't have to. If you want an attorney—"

"It's okay."

"I read the report. It's an amazing story."

"You don't believe me either."

"The report says you had a motive for killing your boyfriend."

"Ex-boyfriend."

"Witnesses say that you were the one who coerced him into the house where he was killed."

"Yes."

"You admitted to the police that you were responsible for your boyfriend's death."

"Ex-boyfriend. Tommy was my ex-boyfriend. And I said I was responsible. I didn't say I actually killed him."

"Where were you when he was killed?"

"I was at home in bed."

"Any witnesses?"

"At two fifteen AM?" Laurel smiled slightly. "No, there weren't any witnesses."

"In what way were you responsible for your boy—excuse me—ex-boyfriend's death?"

"You said you read the report."

"I like to hear the story in your own words."

Laurel sighed deeply and rubbed her eyes again. "Do you believe in ghosts, Mr. Logan?"

"No"

"I do. I believe in ghosts. I didn't believe until last night. I believe now."

"Tell me about it."

"There's a farmhouse out on the county road about ten miles from town. The old Utley place."

"The place where Tommy's body was found?" Logan said.

Laurel nodded.

She was ten when Delores Utley died and even now it was hard to take. Delores had been the girl Laurel had most looked up to, had most wanted to be like. She was smart and she was lovely and she could dance—Delores was the best dancer in Mrs. Cummings Dance School. Laurel had gone to all of her recitals and because Delores danced, Laurel wanted to dance. But more important, Delores always treated Laurel like an equal, like a friend. She never said, "This is the kid I sometimes baby-sit." Instead, Delores would give her a hug or slap her hand in greeting and tell her high school classmates, "Meet my friend, Laurel."

And then she died. The day after Halloween they found her in the Utley home hanging from a rope she had tied herself. At her feet was her boyfriend, his throat slashed so deeply that his head hung backward like the hood of a sweatshirt. According to local gossip, the boyfriend had convinced Delores that he loved her, had taken her virginity and then discarded her. She begged him to come back. He not only refused, he flaunted his new girlfriend in front of her. The police called it murder-suicide, although they never did find the weapon that killed the boy.

The Utley's moved away from the house and it had remained vacant all those years. Rumors circulated that it was haunted. Laurel never believed the rumors. Yet she could not pass the abandoned house without feeling unbearably sad.

Her childhood friend Tommy, however, did believe the rumors. He even claimed to have seen a young woman dressed in white passing before the windows late at night on a number of occasions. Once, when he mustered enough courage to investigate, he said that he came close enough to the house to hear Delores weeping over her lost love. But then he laughed and one never knew if he was serious or not.

By the time they were seniors in high school, Laurel and Tommy had stopped being friends and had become something so much more. Laurel still didn't know how it happened, how they had evolved from boy and girl playing in the backyard to man and woman playing in the bedroom. But she remembered one incident in particular that occurred early in their new relationship.

"Remember Delores Utley?" Tommy had asked her. They were naked in Tommy's bedroom, the house empty except for them.

"Of course."

"She was always looking out for you when we were kids. It was understood, if you mess with Laurel, you answer to Delores."

"I remember."

"After we started dating, she came to me in a dream. She said I should be good to you or else."

"Or else what?"

"She didn't say, but I remember what happened to her boyfriend."

Laurel thought it was a wonderful lie and poked Tommy in the ribs.

"Don't do that," Tommy said. He rolled out of bed and stared down at her. Sweat beaded on his forehead and his body seemed to tremble. "I'm not kidding. She came to me in a dream. More than one dream. She was serious."

It was then that Laurel knew. Tommy really was afraid of ghosts, especially the ghost of Delores Utley.

"Better be nice to me then," she said.

Only Tommy hadn't been nice to her. He professed his undying love for Laurel the night they first made love and then again the night before she left for college in September. Only by the time she returned home for Halloween, he was sleeping with Tiffany Brent who was still in high school. Laurel was stunned by this development and reminded him that he was the only man she had known. He responded by asking how long he was supposed to wait for her.

"More than eight weeks," she told him

The day after Halloween there was a party—beer and a bonfire at the lake. All the kids home from college and those who had stayed in the little town were there. Tommy told stories, as he always did, while Tiffany stared adoringly at him.

"Tommy's afraid of ghosts," Laurel said. That caused several heads to turn. "I mean it. He's terrified of Delores Utley. He claims she comes to him in his dreams. Isn't that right, Tommy?"

"You're crazy," Tommy said.

"How 'bout it, Tiff?" Laurel said. "Has Tommy ever mentioned his fear of ghosts to you?"

Tiffany did the worst thing she could have done to her man. She looked him in the eye and said, "Is it true?"

After that, Laurel didn't have to add much to the conversation to keep it going in the direction she wanted. Eventually, Tommy agreed to spend an entire night in the Utley house if that was what it would take to prove his manhood. He was quite surprised when Laurel jumped up and announced, "No time like the present."

"Now?" he said. As someone correctly noted, it was ten years to the day that Delores had killed her boyfriend and hung herself.

"Right now."

Tommy's fear of being ridiculed was far greater than his fear of the grisly anniversary. He allowed Laurel and a dozen friends to escort him to the house where he bravely kissed Tiffany goodbye, said, "See you in hell," to the cheering crowd and entered the house. Most of the kids lingered to see if he tried to escape; a few tossed rocks on the roof and raked tree branches along the walls. They could hear Tommy shouting from inside, "Real funny, guys." After an hour or so, everyone left.

Early the next morning, Tiffany went to the house to see if Tommy was still there or if he had gone home after the crowd dissipated. She found him, dead, his throat slashed, under the beam where Delores Utley had hung herself a decade earlier. Shortly after, the police questioned Laurel.

"I wanted Delores to kill him," she said. "I was desperate for her to kill him but I never really believed that she would." Laurel covered her face with her hands. "What have I done?"

Logan watched her intently as he leaned against the wall, his arms folded across his chest. He didn't believe her story. His gut and twenty years of experience convinced him that Laurel killed Tommy and set it up so the more gullible would blame Delores Utley. Only he couldn't prove it. The preliminary report he had read earlier said the crime scene investigators were unable to find the murder weapon just as they had been unable to locate it in the first killing. Nor could they uncover a shred of evidence to suggest that anyone had been in the Utley house except Tommy. The case was so weak, Logan was sure if Laurel had asked for an attorney when one had been offered, he would have screamed for her release long before now and he would have gotten it.

Laurel looked up at Logan, studied his expression.

"What will they do to me?" she said.

Logan had no answer. Even if the county attorney believed that the girl had deliberately manipulated Tommy into the house so that Delores would kill him—God, now even he was considering the possibility—what could he do about it? Charge Laurel with conspiracy to commit murder? Call Delores to the stand as a corroborating witness?

The sergeant rapped on the cell door.

"The medical examiner's report just arrived," he said.

Logan excused himself and left the cell. He returned to the front desk and started reading the findings of the Office of the County Coroner. The sergeant glanced at the report over his shoulder.

"So," he said. "Did you hear the girl's story?"

"I heard it."

"What do you think? Do you believe a ghost did it?"

"Do you?"

"You gotta admit, it certainly would make for a novel defense should the matter ever go to trial. Think we'd get on Court TV?"

Logan smiled. He held the report up for the sergeant to see and pointed at the line that read Date and Time of Death.

"I don't believe in ghosts," he said. "Do you want to know what I believe in? I believe in forensic pathology."

A minute later Logan was back in the cell standing before the girl.

"Ms. Clark, I would like to clarify something you said earlier," he said.

"Certainly."

"I asked where you were when Tommy was killed."

"I said I was in bed."

"I asked if there were witnesses."

"I said there weren't any."

"No, you said at two fifteen AM there weren't any witnesses."

"So?"

Logan held up the coroner's report. He was smiling broadly. "How did you know that's when Tommy was killed?"

Laurel didn't hesitate for a moment.

"Because, Mr. Logan," she said, "two fifteen— that's the exact same time when Delores Utley killed her boyfriend ten years ago."

Author's Note: Another contribution for a Minnesota Crime Wave anthology—Fifteen Tales of Murder, Mayhem, and Malice from the Land of Minnesota Nice—*this time with no strings attached. All they wanted was a story that takes place in Minnesota. So I gave them one inspired by a chance encounter I had with a pretty college girl who was giving readings of Tarot cards in a small tent at the Stone Arch Bridge Art Festival along the river in Minneapolis. I asked her if she ever told her customers if the cards said something awful was going to happen. She said, "No one pays ten dollars to hear bad news."*

A Turn of the Card

Probably all of his employees thought he was having an affair, that he had a mistress stashed on the top floor of the apartment complex in downtown Minneapolis overlooking the Mississippi River. Maybe his wife did, too. She had been awfully quarrelsome, lately. He wasn't happy about it. Yet it was better that they believed a lie than knew the truth.

He parked his car at a meter on Washington Avenue and walked to the entrance. The security guards knew him. After all, he had been visiting unit 427 at least once a week for the past two years. Yet they made him sign in, anyway, and called ahead before they granted him access to the elevators. He didn't mind. There were cameras in the elevators, outside the elevators and overlooking all the corridors that led to the lofts. There were even panic buttons spaced out along the corridors. He didn't mind those, either.

He knocked softly when he reached 427. The door was pulled open and a young man stepped back to let him pass.

"Good morning, Mr. G," he said.

"Morning, Joe." Mr. G waited while Joe closed the door before he said, "How is she today?"

"Just great, Mr. G."

"Don't give me that, Joe. I asked you a question."

The young man took a deep breath and answered with the exhale. "She's unhappy, Mr. G. She wants out of here. She wants—well, you know."

Mr. G patted Joe's shoulder.

"I know," he said.

"Want me to take off for a while as usual?"

"Be back in an hour."

"Yes, sir."

Joe slipped on his sports jacket, making sure it covered the Beretta he had holstered behind his right hip before he left the apartment. Mr. G slapped the extra dead bolts into place as soon as Joe left and moved deeper into the apartment. His hand brushed the top of a stuffed chair as he crossed the living room. It was an expensive chair. Hell, everything in the loft was expensive. It had cost him $67,842 to furnish it.

"Good morning, Jill," he called. When there was no answer as he moved into the dining room. "Jillian?"

She stepped through the doorway leading to the kitchen carrying a silver serving tray loaded with cups, saucers, spoons, cream, sugar and ornate coffee pot; moving cautiously as if she were threatened by life's sharp edges. Jillian was young, no more than twenty-two he knew, with golden hair that bounced against her shoulders, a fetching figure and smooth, milky-fresh skin colored with the tint of roses, skin he had seen only in northern girls. Yet it was her eyes that he found most remarkable. They were warm and wide open and so honest that meeting them made a man regret his many sins. And something else: she was the kindest person he had ever met, the epitome of Minnesota Nice.

"We have a French vanilla blend today," she said. "Hope you like it."

"You know I always love your coffee."

She set down the tray and immediately prepared a cup for Mr. G, hesitating before she dumped the second spoonful of sugar into the bowl and giving it a stir.

"You should have less sugar in your diet but I'm tired of arguing about it," Jillian said.

Mr. G smiled as he took the cup and saucer from her outstretched hand. Always thinking of someone else, he thought. He waited while Jillian made her own coffee and then they sat together in the living room. There was some small talk. It bothered Jillian that Mr. G looked so tired these days. He waved her concerns away as he always did.

"How is Joe working out?" he asked.

"I hate him."

"Has he been out of line?"

"No, no. He's—I don't hate him. Joe's been great. Better than the last guy for sure. I just—I hate this. Living like this."

"I'm sorry, Jill. It won't be for much longer."

"That's what you said six months ago. And six months before that. Gene, I feel like a prisoner here, I don't care how much money you're paying me. I want to walk down the street without a bodyguard following me. I want to travel without asking your permission. I want to go back to school. I want to meet men and go out on dates."

"I guess I can't blame you for that, but it's for your own safety. If my competitors knew what you do for me…"

"I know, I know."

"Joe's a good-looking boy."

"C'mon Gene. Joe is terrified of even touching me for fear you'd have him rubbed out. Do gangsters still say that—rubbed out?"

No, they didn't, Mr. G explained, although he was pleased to learn that Joe was keeping his hands to himself. Joe was one of his most trusted employees. 'Course, so was Scott and he lasted all of six days before he started hitting on Jill. Now his job was driving Mr. G's wife. Still, Joe was a young man and Jillian was a young woman and they spent a lot of time together in private—maybe, Mr. G decided, he should remind Joe of his responsibilities before he left.

Jillian set her cup and saucer on the coffee table and stood.

"Should we get to it?" she asked.

Mr. G followed her back into the dining room and sat at the head of the table. Jillian swept the serving tray back into the kitchen. She returned with a glass bowl filled with oil with a small candle floating on top that she set on the buffet and lit with a match. Almost immediately the room was filled with the scent of jasmine. She used the dimmer switch to lower the lights to three-quarters power—setting the mood, she called it. Afterward, she opened a drawer in the buffet and pulled out a deck of Tarot cards wrapped carefully in a red silk scarf. She unwrapped the cards and pulled off the top twenty-two, setting the remaining fifty-six cards near her elbow.

"I think we'll work with the Major Arcana, today," Jillian said as she passed the cards to Mr. G.

The seventy-eight cards in a Tarot deck are divided into two packs: the Major Arcana and the Minor Arcana, the word "arcana" meaning "secret" in Latin. Major Arcana is the trump cards. Each has a title and is numbered in Roman numerals I to XXI with one unnumbered card, The Fool. The Minor cards consist of four suits of thirteen cards each and except for the addition of "knights," most closely resemble everyday playing cards. Mr. G knew this, along with the Egyptian, Greek, Indian and Chinese origins of Tarot cards, because Jillian had carefully explained it all to him—on more than one occasion. Still, he understood none of it, including why she insisted in calling him "the querent," a phrase he disliked immensely. He only knew that it worked.

Jillian had an uncanny ability to predict significant events in his future, often helping him decide between two alternatives. He had not made an important move without secretly consulting her since he found her dressed like a gypsy and working in a tiny booth at the Stone Arch Bridge Art Festival—emphasis on secretly. Mr. G had become the most influential organized crime figure between Chicago and the West Coast and he was within an eyelash of restoring the criminal underworld that had flourished in Minneapolis until Isadore "Kid Cann" Blumenfeld was finally convicted of a felony—after twenty-five tries—in 1961. All he needed was a little more time to solidify his alliance with the Outfit. Yet he knew if his competitors and other business associates discovered how thoroughly dependent he was on this young Tarot card reader, he wouldn't last a week.

Mr. G shuffled the cards—the only time anyone but Jillian was allowed to touch them.

"Start with a general question," Jillian advised.

"Will my present business endeavors continue to be successful?"

Mr. G passed the cards back to Jillian. She dealt the top three cards face down in a row in front of her. He understood after so many readings that they represented his past, present and future. Jillian turned over the first card. It was labeled The World and it was reversed. Upside down cards were usually not desirable, Mr. G knew.

"At its very best, the appearance of The World card signals the arrival of your heart's desire," Jillian said. "So even when it's upside down like this, its reversed interpretation cannot be too negative. It usually means that you have chosen wisely in the past, but you still have a way to go before the promised rewards will be delivered."

She turned over the second card to reveal The Chariot.

"Ahh," Jillian said. "The Chariot signals that there are battles to be fought and considerable odds to overcome and that resilience of character will be needed if you are to achieve a victorious conclusion. But, when preceded by The World, The Chariot indicates that the rewards you'll receive will be considerable, although you will take on some very taxing duties in the near future."

The third card—indicating the future—caused Jillian to frown. It was The Wheel of Fortune and it was upside down.

"The Wheel of Fortune reversed like this means there are unpleasant surprises in store for you," she said. "But Gene, you need to know that it's the nature of the wheel to turn and you will find that eventually things will change for the better. However, when the Wheel of Fortune is paired with the Chariot, urgent decisions will be needed to make your luck certain."

"What urgent decisions?" Mr. G asked.

Jillian grinned at him. He had seen the grin before and knew what it meant—"After all these years you still don't get how this works?"

"All right, all right," Mr. G said. "Deal 'em again. This time use the Minor cards, too."

Jillian joined the two decks together and passed them to Mr. G. He reshuffled them and passed them back.

"What will cause these unpleasant surprises?" he asked.

Jillian dealt the Temperance and Death cards, both reversed, and the ten of Swords. Mr. G knew that the Death card wasn't necessarily a bad thing, although the first time Jillian had dealt it, it scared the hell out of him

"Temperance indicates that you have a rival who competes with you on an emotional and business level; quarrels and strife are likely," Jillian said. "The Death card reversed tells us that drastic changes must be made and when paired with the ten of Swords - Gene, violence comes."

Mr. G stared at the cards for a long time. He was not concerned that there was a rival—"Like that's new," he muttered—or the violence. What concerned him was that the rival was competing with him on an "emotional level." What the hell did that mean, he wondered.

"Another spread?" he asked.

"Of course."

Mr. G reshuffled the cards and passed them over.

"This time be more precise," Jillian said.

"What will be the outcome of the decisions I make?"

Jillian dealt an Ellipse Spread, designed to answer specific questions. The spread was shaped like an arrowhead, with the first and seventh cards at the apexes and the fourth at the point. It expanded the reading, touching on the past, present, future, steps to take, external influence, hopes and fears and final outcome of the situation. The Fool, three of Pentacles, The Moon, seven of Pentacles, King of Pentacles, seven of Swords and five of Swords—Jillian took a deep breath at the sight of the cards and let it out slowly.

"When I first started doing this, I promised myself if I didn't have anything nice to say to the querent, I wouldn't say anything at all," she said.

"I'm not paying you to be coy with me, Jill."

Jillian dealt three more cards—The Lovers reversed, Ace of Pentacles and five of Pentacles—and took another deep breath.

"Okay," she said. "Now that I have these last three cards, I can tell you I was really concerned, Gene. There is a very strong warning in the original reading that somebody is perpetrating some kind of deceit around you which is potentially quite bad for yourself and your wife. However, the last three cards indicate that you are able to take steps to protect yourself, which is great news."

"Tell me about it."

"In the recent past, you took some calculated risks to improve your position on the material front. On the face, things look very successful. At the moment, you seem to be tying up the last few details connected with it. But it looks to me as though you have not been given all the facts you need to make a good decision. I think you and your wife have been deliberately misled. The man represented as the King of Pentacles appears on the surface to be an honest and helpful associate.

However, I am not convinced that he is as straight-forward as he appears. He is definitely a person with his own agenda. These two sevens, they're a little disconcerting, too. The seven of Pentacles tells you that no matter how events may appear, danger lurks and it is important that you be ready to challenge these events through any channel available to you. These last three cards make it clear that as long as you and your wife remain true to each other, you will find the strength to sort things out, although..."

"Although, what?"

"I am concerned by the reversed Lovers. I have no cards here to substantiate what I'm about to say, but the reversed Lovers—Gene, I get the impression that your wife will be more of a hindrance than a help."

Mr. G thought about it for a moment. A hindrance? It was true that they had not been getting along as well lately as they could have, but—he gathered up the cards, reshuffled them, slid the deck in front of Jillian and said, "How will my wife be a hindrance to me?"

Jillian dealt The Moon, Queen of Cups reversed, The Fool, seven of Wands, seven of Cups, nine of Pentacles and The Empress.

"Well?" Mr. G said.

Jillian knew better than to lie to him.

"You have recently discovered some deceit taking place around you," she said. "This appears to be connected to the woman indicated by the Queen of Cups. She's reversed, which indicates—Gene, it indicates a woman who can be immoral and vain, deceitful and perverse, a faithless lover who forces others to indulge her idle whims. However, the Moon can indicate all kinds of deception, including the sort that means things aren't what they seem. Very soon you will be asked to take a risk. This will be quite demanding and you might be tempted to shy away from it. Please don't. Somewhere very close to you is a person who calls himself a friend, but who is running a personal agenda that will do you no good at all. This betrayal will become apparent in the immediate future. And you will be able to pinpoint the individual accurately. Don't be afraid to act. What goes around comes around. Be ready to receive good fortune and happiness. With the Empress in the final position, you'll find love in the air very soon. Just be ready to take the risk when it comes your way."

Mr. G stared at the young woman. God, she was beautiful, he thought. Was she the Empress? No, no, stop it. What are you thinking? This is crazy. These cards are wrong.

"Jill, you're telling me that my wife and one of my people are conspiring against me."

"I'm not telling you anything. The cards…"

"The cards? You're expecting me to believe the cards?"

"You always have."

"I want a second reading. Second reading."

Mr. G gathered the cards, shuffled them, gave the deck to Jillian and asked, "How will my wife be a hindrance to me?"

Jillian dealt an Ace of Disks, The Fool, Lust, The Tower, Justice, The Sun and The Lovers.

"Again we see uncertainty about something you have recently discovered, with the Tower indicating shock and sudden violence. There is a mention of great and irreversible change, but the same indications that events will very soon re-shape themselves and allow you a more happy and positive period."

"I don't believe it," Mr. G said. "I don't believe any of it."

Jillian shrugged as she gathered up her Tarot cards and re-wrapped them in the red silk scarf.

"The cards say that all will be revealed to you in the immediate future," she said.

"What's that supposed to mean?"

There was a soft rapping on the door. Joe had returned as instructed—he had a key, yet never let himself into the loft while Mr. G was in residence. Mr. G rose from his chair and began his departure. Jillian called to him.

"Gene?"

"What?"

"Please be careful."

He nodded at her and yanked the door open, startling Joe and causing him to take a step backward. Mr. G set a hand on the young man's shoulder. There was nothing affectionate about the gesture.

"Listen to me," he said. "Are you listening?"

"Yes, sir."

"Anything happens to that girl in there better happen to you, first. Understand?"

"Yes, sir."

Mr. G retreated from the building, pausing only to sign himself out at the security desk. All the while he considered what the Tarot cards had told him. His wife cheating on him? Sure, they seemed to be going through a rough patch, but that happens to every marriage from time to time, right? And yeah, lately she had been spending a lot of time with her friends. Still, conspiring to betray him with someone in his organization? The cards had always been true in the past but—no, no, no. Not this time. Jillian had screwed up. Or maybe she was just pissed off because he kept her a virtual prisoner in her ivory tower. She had told him once that a true and accurate reading required a calm system and a clear mind. You need to be relaxed. Did Jillian look relaxed to you? Well, yeah, he decided, she did. Yet the cards were wrong. They had to be. After all, who could his wife be involved with? Her driver Scott? Granted, he was unable keep his hands off Jillian...

Mr. G stopped on the sidewalk several yards short of his car. "I don't believe it," he shouted even as he pointed his remote control at the vehicle and pressed the button that opened his locks.

The car exploded.

The force of the blast threw him up against the building.

This betrayal will become apparent in the immediate future, Jillian had said. It was the only thought he held for several moments.

One security guard had hurried to the site of the explosion. The rest had remained at their posts on high alert. They were good boys, Mr. G decided; the kind of boys he wanted in his organization. He returned to 427 without bothering to wait for the police and pounded on the door. It was cautiously opened by Joe who said "Hey, Mr. G. Did you forget something?" Mr. G ignored him, pushing deep into the loft.

"Jill," he called. "Jill, Jill." When she appeared he said, "I need another reading."

He sat at the dining room table in a way that indicated he expected no argument. Jillian gave him one, anyway.

"It doesn't work that way, Gene. You know that. The rule is to wait until circumstances in your life have made a definite change before consulting the cards on the same issue."

"Someone just tried to assassinate me. They put a bomb in my car. How is that for a definite change?"

Without another word, Jillian produced the Tarot cards, unwrapped the scarf and set them in front of the querent. She did not lower the lights or burn jasmine. Mr. G shuffled the cards and passed them to her.

"How should I deal with the betrayal of my wife and my employee?" he asked.

"Jeezuz," a voice said behind him. Mr. G turned to look. Joe immediately left the room.

Jillian dealt the cards in the Ellipse Spread: The Magician, Death, five of Wands, three of Wands, The Lovers, eight of Disks and The Star.

"You've recently suffered a shocking blow in both an emotional and business relationship," she said. "You seem to be expressing a deep sense of distrust and disappointment. You also seem shaken and disbelieving. In the imminent future there will be a certain amount of conflict, both inner and from outside. You will sometimes feel overwhelmed by the enormity of the events that have taken place and uncertain of your ability to deal with them. I think you will also feel bitter and angry, but if you accept that you're bound to be feeling hurt and then just engage with your hurt, you'll soon be kinder to yourself as you come to grips with this situation. It is important that you make no compromises during this time. You must be true to yourself. You must follow your code. You'll feel stronger and more clear if you do. In a short time, decisions will be made that will begin to straighten this situation out. Again, it is important that you take care of yourself and make sure your emotional and business needs are attended to. The final card in your reading, in my opinion, is the very best card in the deck. The Star. It promises that your dreams will be fulfilled, your hopes realized and your aspirations satisfied. It's a beautiful card."

That was all Mr. G needed to hear. He stood abruptly. Jillian also rose from her chair. He took her face in the palms of his hands. He felt like kissing her. He had never done that before. Hell, he thought, he had never even touched her. But that was going to change. Everything was going to change, and quickly. The future she had promised was so wonderful he couldn't wait for it to begin.

Mr. G released the young woman and stepped back.

"Thank you," he said.

He left the loft.

Three days later, Mr. G's wife and her driver were killed in a traffic accident. Or so it was assumed at the time. Acting on an anonymous tip, the police soon discovered the truth and Mr. G was arrested and charged with two counts of first-degree murder. Bail was refused. Joe was the one who broke the news to Jillian.

"He thought his dreams were about to be fulfilled," he said.

"I can't help it if Gene believed all that crap."

"I don't get it. You told me you weren't psychic, that the only reason you were reading Tarot cards at the art fair in the first place was to make some extra money for college."

"That's right," Jillian said.

"Yet everything you told Mr. G in the past two years came true."

"Nah. He subconsciously manipulated events so it seemed to him that my predictions were always accurate even when they weren't. He talked himself into it. That's what true believers do. My old psychology professor called it confirmation bias."

Joe stepped up to Jillian and wrapped his arms around her waist.

"So, now that you can go anywhere you want, where do you want to go?" he asked.

Jillian draped her arms around Joe's neck.

"I thought we'd stay in," she said. "After all, I never did thank you properly for setting the bomb."

Author's Note: When Otto Penzler, the renowned mystery author, editor, publisher, columnist and bookstore owner calls, you answer. He said he was editing an anthology of crime stories and he wanted me to contribute. I said sure. He said there would be ninety other writers involved. I said ninety? He said the anthology would be called KWIK KRIMES and each story would be told in a swift one thousand words or less! Are you in? I said umm, okay... Writing a complete story in less than a thousand words? Not as easy as it looks.

The Blackmailer Wanted More

He heard the fear in her voice the moment she recognized his.

"No phone calls," she said. "We agreed to communicate only through chat rooms."

He assured her that it was an emergency and directed her to a park they both knew.

"Are we in trouble, Kevin?" she asked.

"Yes, Emma. I'm sorry."

He was sorry, too. Sorry for her, but mostly sorry for himself. A year ago, Kevin was named the youngest vice president in the firm. Old man Torrance himself had taken notice and often invited Kevin and his beautiful bride Lisa to gatherings at his fabulous estate—that's where he was introduced to Emma, Torrance's long-legged trophy wife. Unfortunately, he and Lisa had drifted apart mostly because of the grueling hours Kevin worked and the long trips Torrance sent him on. They hadn't enjoyed sex in weeks. Kevin decided if she was going to be that way... He met Emma in the elevator. She was willing, so he slept with her that evening. Kevin meant for it to be a one-night stand, something to remind him that he was still desirable to women. Yet he saw her again the following week and then a third time three days later—never at the same place twice. They had been very careful

Emma was waiting for him on the park bench. He could see the anxiety on her face. He answered her nervous questions by presenting a letter that he discovered in his mailbox. "I know about your affair" it said and "I will tell Torrance" unless "I'm paid $10,000." The letter was accompanied by three laser-printed photographs. The first was taken through a bedroom window and showed Kevin and Emma embracing. They were embracing in the second photo as well; although Emma's yellow sundress was now lying at their feet. In the third photo, Emma's bra and panties had joined the sundress.

"What are we going to do?" she asked.

"Pay him. He's threatening to take away my wife, my job, probably my career. What would you lose?"

"Everything. The way our pre-nup is written and Roger, his temper—you can't imagine his temper. And his kids... What was I thinking sleeping with you?"

"Good question." Kevin was attempting to sound blasé, yet was surprised at the ache he felt. He liked Emma and thought she liked him. "I can come up with five thousand."

"I can find the rest, but what if he wants more?" Emma asked.

Turned out, the blackmailer did want more. Kevin had followed his instructions impeccably— the cash was sealed inside a white envelope with "Room 1242" written on it and brought to the front desk of a downtown hotel. Kevin gave the envelope to a clerk. He tried to learn who was staying in 1242, but the hotel had a policy against revealing information about its guests. Two weeks later, Kevin received a second letter. The instructions were identical to the first except for a change in room number and hotel.

"What are we going to do?" This time it was Kevin who asked the question. "I can't keep withdrawing five grand in cash from our accounts without Lisa finding out."

"Sooner or later he'll betray us, anyway," Emma said. "I know he will."

"Maybe we should just go to our spouses and explain…"

"No, no, no, no, no. When I married Roger everyone accused me of being a gold digger, a blonde bimbo from the wrong side of the tracks who was using her looks and sex to snare a rich husband. It wasn't true. I married Roger because I genuinely loved him. There's no way he's leaving me. No way I'm leaving him. They were right about one thing, though. I am from the wrong side of the tracks. I know people."

"What's that mean?"

Emma glanced cautiously around her. When she was sure no one was watching, she dipped into her bag and produced a white envelope. She told Kevin to take it and follow the blackmailer's instructions. Roger knew what it was, yet asked anyway.

"It's a letter bomb," Emma said. "We're lucky because the blackmailer expects the envelope to be thick with cash. It allows us to pack it with more explosives. Otherwise it would just pop and flash like a firework."

Kevin held the bomb as if taking a deep breath would be enough to set it off. Emma told him to relax, but he couldn't. He gave her a long list of reasons why they shouldn't do this.

"We have no choice," Emma said. "Besides, it's the blackmailer's fault. He started it." Kevin still wasn't convinced. She kissed him, kissed him passionately. "Do this and I'll sleep with you one last time," she said.

An hour later, Kevin delivered the envelope to the downtown hotel designated by the blackmailer. The next day, he was arrested for murder.

The case was smartly presented. First, the prosecutor described how Kevin had withdrawn five thousand dollars in cash to buy the bomb. Next, he presented security footage of him handing the envelope to a hotel desk clerk who passed it to a bellhop. The bellhop testified that he carried it to Room 4786 and gave it to Roger Torrance. Finally, the medical examiner explained how Torrance opened the letter, detonating the bomb that killed him as well as the woman he had been meeting at the hotel once a week for six months—Kevin's wife, Lisa.

Kevin blamed Emma. Emma denied everything and since the letters and photographs had somehow gone missing, Kevin couldn't even prove they had an affair much less that it was she who plotted the crime.

"I loved my husband," a teary-eyed Emma testified at a pre-trial hearing. "It broke my heart when I learned he was cheating on me."

Kevin believed her. In the end, he exchanged a guilty plea for a chance at parole in two hundred ten months. That same week, Emma inherited half of her husband's estate.

"The Blackmailer Wanted More" Copyright ©2013 by David Housewright. First published in *Kwik Krimes*, Thomas & Mercer. Edited by Otto Penzler.

ABOUT THE AUTHOR

A reformed newspaper reporter and ad man, David Housewright has published 16 crime novels including THE DEVIL MAY CARE. His book PENANCE earned the 1996 Edgar Award for Best First Novel from the Mystery Writers of America as well as a Shamus nomination from the Private Eye Writers of America. PRACTICE TO DECEIVE (1998), JELLY'S GOLD (2010), and CURSE OF THE JADE LILY (2013) have each won Minnesota Book Awards. Housewright's short stories have appeared in publications as diverse as Ellery Queen's Mystery Magazine and True Romance as well as mystery anthologies including SILENCE OF THE LOONS, TWIN CITIES NOIR and ONCE UPON A CRIME. He was elected President of the Private Eye Writers of America in 2014. In addition, Housewright has taught novel-writing courses at the University of Minnesota and Loft Literary Center in Minneapolis, MN.

http://www.davidhousewright.com/

OTHER TITLES FROM DOWN AND OUT BOOKS

See www.DownAndOutBooks.com for complete list

By J.L. Abramo
Catching Water in a Net
Clutching at Straws
Counting to Infinity
Gravesend
Chasing Charlie Chan
Circling the Runway (*)

By Trey R. Barker
2,000 Miles to Open Road
Road Gig: A Novella
Exit Blood

By Richard Barre
The Innocents
Bearing Secrets
Christmas Stories
The Ghosts of Morning
Blackheart Highway
Burning Moon
Echo Bay
Lost (*)

Rob Brunet
Stinking Rich (*)

By Milton T. Burton
Texas Noir

By Reed Farrel Coleman
The Brooklyn Rules

By Tom Crowley
Vipers Tail
Murder in the Slaughterhouse (*)

By Frank De Blase
Pine Box for a Pin-Up
Busted Valentines and Other Dark Delights
The Cougar's Kiss (*)

By Les Edgerton
The Genuine, Imitation, Plastic Kidnapping (*)

By A.C. Frieden
Tranquility Denied
The Serpent's Game

By Jack Getze
Big Numbers
Big Money
Big Mojo (*)

By Keith Gilman
Bad Habits

(*)—Coming Soon

OTHER TITLES FROM DOWN AND OUT BOOKS

See www.DownAndOutBooks.com for complete list

By Terry Holland
An Ice Cold Paradise
Chicago Shiver

By Darrel James, Linda O.
Johsonton & Tammy Kaehler
(editors)
Last Exit to Murder

By David Housewright &
Renée Valois
The Devil and the Diva

By David Housewright
Finders Keepers
Full House

By Jon Jordan
Interrogations

By Jon & Ruth Jordan
Murder and Mayhem in Muskego
(Editors)

By Bill Moody
Czechmate
The Man in Red Square
Solo Hand (*)
The Death of a Tenor Man (*)
The Sound of the Trumpet (*)
Bird Lives! (*)

By Gary Phillips
The Perpetrators
Scoundrels (Editor)
Treacherous: Griffters, Ruffians and Killers (*)

Robert J. Randisi
Upon My Soul
Souls of the Dead (*)
Envy the Dead (*)

By Lono Waiwaiole
Wiley's Lament
Wiley's Shuffle
Wiley's Refrain
Dark Paradise

By Vincent Zandri
Moonlight Weeps (*)

(*)—Coming Soon

Made in the USA
Lexington, KY
30 January 2015